THE PEACEFUL WARRIOR

NAVY SEAL ROMANCE

DANIEL BANNER

ALSO BY DANIEL BANNER

Navy SEAL Romance Series

The Peaceful Warrior

The Captivating Warrior

Park City Firefighter Romance Series

Two Hearts Rescue

A Perfect Rescue

Rescue and Redemption

Park City Firefighter Romance Series: Station Two

Sparks Will Fly

Kisses and Commitment Series

How to Find a Keeper

My Heart Channel Romance Series

9 Reasons to Fall in Love

1

---

ust boarded. Departing soon. See you tomorrow! Daisy Close
added an emoji of a train and an excited smiley then
pressed send on the text to Maia. Tucking her phone away,
she glanced out the window at the busy platform, and then
pulled out her well-worn copy of *Jane Eyre*. An actual paperback
book. For a minute she just flipped the pages, savoring the feel of
them along her thumb. For a woman who worked with books—
editing novels for a living—it was a rare occasion to pick up a paperback and read for pleasure. She was going to have to get some work
done during the 36-hour train trip to Seattle to visit her old college
roommate. But for a few moments at least, she planned to indulge in
one of her all-time favorites.

The coach car of the train was much roomier than coach on an
airplane, with only two seats on each side of the aisle and the ability
to recline almost completely flat. Taking a long train ride had always
been on her unofficial bucket list and here she was, about to depart.
For now, the seat next to her was empty, but in the next five minutes,
or at any of the twenty or so stops along the way, that could change.

Overhead announcements echoed through the car, but Daisy was already getting lost in her book. She was vaguely aware of the other passengers as they filed down the aisle stashing luggage and filling in seats. With a gentle lurch, the train started rolling. If it hadn't been for the initial movement and the view of the Los Angeles Union Station passing outside, she wouldn't know they were moving. The train was much smoother than she expected. And the most serendipitous aspect of the whole thing, she had the row to herself. Nearly every seat in the car was filled and she had two seats for her little old self. Even more room to spread out.

"Wanna let me squeeze past," said a man at her shoulder.

And just like that, Daisy's luck was shattered. She never should have gotten her hopes up so soon.

Returning her seat to the upright position, Daisy stood and moved into the aisle, facing forward to avoid seeing the guy who would be her neighbor. With any luck he'd be handsome, strong, and have nothing to do for the next 36 hours other than discuss the classics with her.

She turned to see her new boyfriend and saw ... something else completely. The man was 30-ish, maybe five years older than her, but that was where the compatibility ended. He was unshaven—not sporting a little stubble, which she didn't like anyway, but downright scruffy. It had probably been as long since he shaved as it had since he'd brushed his hair. And probably longer since he washed his shirt, judging by the food stains on it. Even with the wide aisles and spacious accommodations, he was going to have a hard time squeezing between the seats. Daisy wondered if his girth would spill over and fill part of her seat.

He grunted at her as he lifted one of his backpacks on to her seat and, completely blocking the aisle, started sorting the contents. Daisy couldn't tell what he was saying. She could only assume he was prepping his bags to put one in the overhead storage and keep one at his seat with him.

So much for her travel boyfriend. Keeping things positive, she imagined a backstory for him. He had probably spent the last year sequestered in a ... leper colony? Did they still have those? Sure, why not? And now he was taking some well-deserved time off for himself. That sounded right.

Daisy smiled at him, and took inventory of the rest of the car as her seatmate repacked his belongings. She picked up a rank odor—tofu or blue cheese maybe—and looked around to see which of the other passengers had brought stinky food with them. The coach ticket did not include any meals, so most of the people in her car would be eating food they'd packed along with them.

The people around Daisy were intent on their phones and tablets and naps. No one had food out.

Oh no. That wasn't food. The smell was being emitted by the man she was about to spend a day and a half with. Her stomach turned over at the image of remnants of rotting flesh from the imaginary leper colony.

Sometimes her active imagination was a curse. How quickly her dream vacation had been chopped up, shoved into the disposal, and blended into a million slimy pieces.

Daisy turned her back on her failed boyfriend and saw the door from the next car slide open.

At the far end of the car, her real travel boyfriend was stepping through the door. Tall, clean cut, bold bearing, and as handsome as Mr. Rochester was plain. Why couldn't *that* guy get stuck next to her? Judging by his perfectly cut suit—on a body she couldn't see much of, but appeared to be perfectly proportioned—he wasn't riding in the cheap coach seats. Daisy's eyes started fluttering like some silly girl before she got them under control.

The guy, her new boyfriend, was scanning the train car as if he was playing Where's Waldo. The grin on his lips seemed to say, *Life is good.* His eyes slid over the contents of the car without stopping on anything ... until they caught on Daisy's eyes, where he paused like a sprinkler reaching the end of its swivel.

We met on a train. When I looked into his eyes, everyone else on the train evaporated like mist. The aisle was a mile long, but as we stood still, locked in a gaze, the magnetism between us brought us speeding together as the distance shrunk in an instant. He put his hands on my shoulders and—

Her boyfriend pulled his gaze away, continuing his scan of the compartment and giving Daisy whiplash.

Sometimes she wrote little snippets of her life—okay, snippets of the fantasy she wished was her life—inside her head, and she'd been way too deep in that one. It came from editing multiple novels every week, analyzing the love story, the setting, the prose, and overall the romanticism of it all. This perfect specimen of a man walking through the door just when her other travel boyfriend had gone up in smoke had caught her way off guard and she found herself catching her breath.

Daisy checked behind her and saw that her former boyfriend had set up a yard sale on her seat. She wasn't getting in any time soon, so she turned back to the more pleasant view.

Apparently her new boyfriend had finished looking for whatever he was seeking and had stepped aside. A woman and a little girl stepped out from behind him and started up the aisle.

A little family.

Well, that was low of her. She'd never claimed a guy who was with his family as her imaginary boyfriend before.

The poised, perfect woman led the way up the aisle and Daisy looked for somewhere she could curl up and die from shame, but there was nowhere but the aisle to do so. Daisy just waited and tried to keep her blush down as the family walked up the aisle toward her.

The wife carried herself with an air of confidence, and was as perfectly put-together as the man. Straight, dark hair, makeup so flawless it looked like she'd been born with it, and grace that seemed inhuman on a moving train. A large Hermes bag hung on her shoulder.

In romance novels, a scene when a future romantic couple met for the first time was called a meet cute. And now Daisy was face-to-face with the woman after she'd imaginarily meet-cuted her husband right in front of her.

"Hi," said Daisy, angling her body to hide her blush and also allow the woman to see past her to the roadblock.

The woman smiled back and said, "Hello." Oh, a British accent. So both of these people were ideal specimens.

From behind the mom, a cute little towheaded girl leaned out and said, "Hi, what's your name?"

"Daisy Close. What's yours?"

The girl was tiny enough to squeeze past her mom and step up to Daisy. She was maybe five years old. With a crooked finger, she summoned Daisy down to her level.

The darling little girl reminded Daisy of a straight-haired Shirley Temple. She bent down to come face to face with her.

"Nice to meet you, Ms. Close. I'm Pasha," whispered the girl. "I'm not s'pose to say that too loud though."

"That's a very pretty name," said Daisy quietly, wondering why the girl didn't have a British accent.

Pasha was missing a front tooth, so she spoke with a bit of a lisp. "My real name's Appassionata."

That sounded familiar and it only took Daisy a second to place it. "Is that from something called Li'l Abner?"

The girl's eyes lit up. "Yeah! That's what my mommy told me!"

"Guess what," said Daisy conspiratorially. "My real name's Daisy Mae. That's from Li'l Abner too."

Pasha's eyes lit up like she was talking to a Disney princess. "That means we're like sisters! I always wanted a sister."

That was super sweet, but Daisy had mixed feelings about her own sister. "Well now you have one. And so you should call me Daisy."

Pasha's parents were quiet, allowing their daughter to make new friends while they waited for Daisy's seat to clear so she could clear the aisle. Mom just looked down patiently. Dad watched much more intently as if he was worried Daisy meant his daughter harm, but every two seconds or so his eyes darted to another part of the car.

Daisy wondered what his hurry was. Everyone on the train was relaxed and ready for a long, laid-back trip, but this guy had a hard time standing still and waiting for the aisle to open.

Behind Daisy, her seatmate started having a coughing fit. For about half a minute he coughed into a paper napkin. Maybe it was a tuberculosis sanatorium where he'd been living and volunteering for the last twelve months. When he was done coughing, he appeared out of breath and a little sweaty.

"Do you want something to drink?" asked Daisy, touching his shoulder. He nodded so she pulled a bottle of water out of her carryon.

He rasped, "Thanks," then cracked it open and started draining it.

The dad of the group was staring at Daisy, distracted from his inspection of the train car. Everyone else was looking at the man, probably wondering if he'd keel over. But not the hot dad. It was like he couldn't believe Daisy was engaging with the man, but what else was she supposed to do? She could afford a few bucks to replace the bottled water and kindness didn't cost anything.

Realizing he'd been staring, the dad went back to scanning everything. Daisy looked and saw her seatmate squeeze in front of her seat and plop down heavily into his own. He immediately claimed all of the armrest as well as part of her seat.

Good thing Daisy was slender and didn't need all of her space. She was happy to give up what she wasn't using. Daisy took her seat and said, "It was very nice to meet you, sister."

"We're going to see the last car, but they told me it has passengers in it. Is it still called a caboose?" The little girl was in no rush to move on.

Daisy leaned on the armrest by the aisle. "I don't know. I've never been on a train before."

"I ride trains all the time," said Pasha. "Next week—"

"Pasha," said her dad gently.

"Oh." The girl obviously wasn't supposed to say what she'd been about to say so she changed tracks. "I know everything about trains."

"That's good," said Daisy. "Now I know who to ask when I have questions."

"We'll be right back after we find out if there's a caboose on this train. You should come to the parlour car with us when we come back."

Daisy had read about a lounge car and a Pacific Parlour car where people could hang out and get a better view of the beautiful scenery. But she was still a little fuzzy on exactly what amenities were available to coach passengers.

"Maybe," said Daisy. "Ask me when you come back this way."

"Okay. Bye, big sister."

"Bye, little sister."

Pasha went skipping up the aisle. Mom mouthed, *thank you* as she followed her. The dad paused momentarily and examined the seating arrangement in Daisy's row. The guy in the next seat over was already busy with a movie on a tablet—no headphones—and a bag of chips, half of which appeared to be ending up in his facial hair and on his shirt. The dad looked like he was about to speak to Daisy, but instead, just gave her a wink and a smile then snapped forward like he was pulled by an invisible leash attached to his family.

Daisy just stared at him, stunned. Was that a thank-you wink? Judging by the butterflies that took flight in her stomach, it sure didn't feel like that. Daisy had no interest in flirting with a married man; she would never go there. But her body didn't seem to be listening to her mind and her heart was beating like a bass drum.

Why couldn't a hot, *single* guy wink at her like that? Unattached. Available. Oh well. Daisy sighed and went back to her book, leaning onto her armrest and encroaching into the aisle as the guy next to her was encroaching into her personal space.

It was going to be a long trip.

Before she had made it through an entire page, Pasha was tapping her on the arm.

"Hi, big sister."

"You're back already? Is it a caboose?"

Pasha sighed. In her cute little lisp she said, "It's kinda confusing if you don't know a lot about trains. Come with us to the parlour car and I'll 'splain it."

The idea of sitting anywhere besides her assigned seat appealed to Daisy. But she didn't trust the five-year old's invitation that a coach passenger was really allowed up there. "Is it okay with your parents?"

Without looking up, Pasha said, "My parents said I can make friends on the train as long as I stay with Miss Dee and Cannon."

Who? wondered Daisy. She looked up at the mom who picked up on her confusion.

In a confidential voice, the mom said, "We aren't Miss Pasha's parents. I'm Miss Dee, and this is Cannon." Her refined English accent was straight out of a British Royalty movie.

The guy—who was *not* Dad—was leaning around Miss Dee. His smile had turned somewhat amused, but he didn't speak. Wait, that meant ... the wink .... Oh! Daisy gulped. So he was available on the boyfriend buffet again, and Daisy immediately claimed him as her new fake boyfriend again. She forced herself to drag her eyes away from him and look back at Pasha. "Is it okay with Miss Dee and Cannon if I go with you?"

"Anyone's allowed to go," said Pasha. Then to Miss Dee she said, "May she come with us, Miss Dee?"

Cannon was looking at Miss Dee, waiting for her to answer. Was it Daisy's imagination or was he looking at Miss Dee with the same hopeful expression that Pasha was?

"Of course she can," said Miss Dee. In a whisper that the little girl couldn't hear, she said to Daisy, "If you want to read there, I suggest going on your own. If you fancy a board game, you're welcome to come with us."

That was enough for Daisy. Leaving her book on her seat, she grabbed her purse and stood in the aisle, a little lightheaded at the thought of Cannon so close to her. She looked up into his deep emerald eyes, and just about went away into another fantasy. She cleared her throat and said to Pasha, "Show me the way, little sis."

Pasha started up the aisle, then paused and turned sideways. Miss Dee stepped past Daisy and Pasha, taking the lead. "Go ahead of me," said Pasha. "I'll be right behind you."

As Daisy took the directed place in line, she heard Cannon tell the girl, "That's my smart girl." Out of the corner of her eye she saw Pasha and Cannon bump fists.

Their relationship was boggling. These people were obviously rich, and becoming richer with everything Daisy learned about them. He could be like a chauffeur. No, that didn't make any sense. Butler? Did a rich girl need a butler on a train? He didn't seem like a butler. How about a valet? In her head she pronounced it with a hard 't' like she'd heard on a British TV show. Yeah, that was probably it because she really had no idea what a valet did, and she had no idea what her travel boyfriend Cannon's role was.

Daisy itched to pull out her phone and look up that word. The editor in her hated not knowing it, but she resisted the urge.

When they reached the front of the car, Miss Dee stepped aside as did Pasha and Daisy after they passed Miss Dee. Cannon took the lead and pushed a big rectangular inset button on the door and it slid open. He stepped into the breezeway between cars and hit a similar activator on the next car and that door slid open too.

"Do I go?" Daisy asked her little sis. There weren't any big gaps where the train cars met that necessarily looked dangerous, but Daisy pictured the train shifting and her putting her foot into a gap and having it pinched right off. She'd never gone between train cars in her life and didn't want to look like an idiot in front of her on-again mock boyfriend.

"Yep," said Pasha. "The doors stay open long enough for all of us to go through. I was scared my first time too."

With a brave little smile on her face, Daisy stepped through one doorway, over the creaking connections between two train cars, and into a completely different car than her coach car. There were some curved couches with small tables, some soft chairs with armrests, and huge windows along both sides of the train to maximize the view.

Cannon fell to the rear, and they all followed Miss Dee into one of the curved couches. Miss Dee and Cannon settled on the ends with Pasha and Daisy in the middle. They'd spread out as much as the couch allowed, but because of the curve, her knee was like an inch away from her travel boyfriend's knee.

I knew if our legs touched, the spark would be obvious to everyone within a mile. It would spark a fire that could only be quenched by a kiss—

"Do you like it?" asked Pasha.

Startled, Daisy looked around. There was space here and great viewing windows, plus the hottest guy on the train. And nothing smelled bad. What was not to like?

"I love it," she answered, still reeling a bit from the nearness of her travel boyfriend. She needed a safe topic of conversation. "Are we out of the city already?" The train was passing through a desert area with low trees. Here and there she spotted a ranch home, some trails, and horse corrals.

"This is Los Padres National Forest," explained Cannon, only glancing out of the window for a moment. His voice was firm, but not harsh. Confident and ... contented.

"May we please play Connect Four?" Pasha said to Miss Dee.

"That sounds wonderful," said Miss Dee, opening the large bag and digging in to it.

To Daisy, Pasha said, "This is a game for only two players, big sister. I'll play against Miss Dee, then I'll play against you cause you'll know how to play by watching us."

Daisy already knew how to play, but she was happy to go along with her little train guide's plan, especially if it left her to focus on her hot boyfriend.

Miss Dee set a travel-sized version of the game on the small table and those two turned their attention to it. Even though Daisy was more or less alone with her travel boyfriend, she didn't feel like he was really with her. His attention roved from Pasha to the rest of the train and back, only settling on Daisy as often as it did on the door at the far end of the car. She might as well have been another empty chair. So if he wasn't even interested in looking at her when she was right in front of his face, what had been up with that wink?

It was back to Sterling all over again. Daisy was nothing more than the background to Cannon's life, just like she'd been to Sterling. And to think she'd wasted years with Sterling, hoping and expecting him to start putting her first once his life became less hectic. Why did fate keep putting guys like that in front of her?

Stop it, she told herself. *He isn't your real boyfriend, just a guy on a train who's nice enough to let you hang out with his weird little non-family so you don't have to sit next to the leper colony sanitarium rescue worker.*

"So what's your deal?" she playfully asked her fake boyfriend. "If you're not dad, and Miss Dee isn't mom, then what?"

Pasha answered for him. "Miss Dee's my nanny." She kept her

eyes on the game, but was clearly talking to Daisy. "She's the best nanny I ever had. Sometimes I call her Nanny Dee."

That made sense. Daisy probably should have figured that one out, but Miss Dee seemed more like royalty than a nanny. And that still didn't answer the Cannon question.

"So, the nanny job's already taken. What do you do?"

"Cannon's here because he's my best friend," said Pasha without looking back. There was no joking or sarcasm in her voice; she really meant it and it about made Daisy's heart melt.

Daisy raised an eyebrow at him, expecting elaboration, but Cannon just nodded agreement and she could see the proud look on his face. For just a second he held her gaze, then it slid back to his examination of everything else in the parlour car, and he did so just in time. In the spell of his emerald eyes, she'd been about to sink into another one of her silly fantasy rants, and if that happened, she could easily end up hypnotized by him and staring dreamily into those smoking hot eyes.

He broke the spell further by speaking. "I'm just here to make sure Pasha's travel between her parents goes smoothly."

"So you're some kind of valet?"

His smile took on that amused quality again. Daisy didn't feel like she was being mocked, but she could tell he found something funny.

"You just have a good time in life, don't you?" she asked. "You've had that life-is-good smile on your face since I saw you."

"You said it. Life is good."

"Excuse me," said Pasha. She had her hands in her lap like a lady but had turned her body to face them. "If you're going to have a conversation, would you please mind sitting over there?" She signaled to the soft chairs across the aisle. "Nanny Dee's a Connect Four master. She studied Connect Four in college. I need'a concentrate if I'm gonna beat her."

There was that amused twist to his smile again. Daisy was trying to suppress a giggle at the girl's cute little manners.

"Sure thing, Pash." Cannon stood and extended an arm, inviting Daisy to go first.

"Thank you," said Pasha, turning back to her game.

"She did say *please*," whispered Daisy as she passed Cannon and moved to sit in the swiveling armchair in the corner.

"Mind switching?" asked Cannon, gently catching her by the arm. His hand was strong, she could tell, but he only touched her with enough of his strength for her to notice.

Wait! What did he just say? Mind-switching? Did he know that she was going away in her mind, switching between fantasy and real world? Was that why he had that smile like he knew something?

"No, I'm right here. I'm not ... Wait, what do you mean?" She stayed put. She didn't want him to take his hand away and she was tempted to stand there, blocking the chair he wanted for as long as possible, breathing in his light leather cologne smell.

"I just ..." Now he was stalling, confused or off-balance. He looked down at his hand on her arm and startled. "I was wondering if you'd mind switching seats."

"Oh! Would I mind switching seats? I thought you meant was I going somewhere—" Daisy stopped talking and settled in to the chair alongside the one her fake boyfriend wanted. She had almost admitted she was having all sorts of cheesy fantasies about him.

In a very controlled way, he took the seat, looking at her some-what suspiciously, but still with that gorgeous smile on his face. After a few intense seconds, he looked away and ran his surveillance over the entire car again, the focus being on Pasha. Or maybe Miss Dee. Now that Daisy noticed, she couldn't tell which of them he was obsessed with. He'd gone far enough to butt into her seat to get a better view of one of them. If Daisy was a guy, she'd have a hard time keeping her eyes off of Miss Dee as well.

Whichever it was that he was obsessing over, Daisy felt very second-place. It was a good thing they weren't trying to real date or anything because this fake boyfriend of hers had already struck out. When Daisy did get involved again, she would be number one in her man's world, not number two, ten, or any other number. In the meantime, Cannon was fun to be around and so, so easy on the eyes.

Just thinking about how close they were on their nearby seats made her mouth go dry. She said, "You never told me what was in that smile. Something was extra good there for a second."

"Oh, that," said Cannon. "You got me. A valet is a gentleman's manservant."

"Huh. I didn't know that." Daisy filed that away for future use. Eventually one of her authors would throw a valet in one of her books and she'd be ready to show off her big brain when that happened. In the meantime, she was impressed with Cannon's big brain. "Is there an equivalent for a small female person's manservant?"

That got him, and his eyebrows lowered as he considered.

"I got it," said Daisy. "You're a young lady's maid."

A laugh broke from his controlled persona, and Daisy knew she'd earned it. For as happy as her new fake boyfriend was, he was also all business, and he quickly reeled in the laugh. Daisy had heard it, however, and it made her insides all happy to know she'd pulled that out of him.

"Yep, that's it," he nodded. "I'm a lady's maid."

"A lady's maid and also ... a security guy?" If he wasn't security, Daisy couldn't figure out what he could be, but he just didn't have that glare and the intimidating presence she'd expect. Maybe she was thinking of bouncers at a club instead of professional bodyguards. Did people really travel with personal bodyguards? Was a train ride dangerous enough to need one? This wasn't some movie with people lurking on top of the train just waiting to grab Pasha as soon as Cannon blinked. And besides, who would want to hurt that little angel?

Cannon lifted one shoulder in a shrug. "Something like that."

She examined him further, taking in his Cole Haan shoes, perfectly pressed suit, precise haircut, and just his strong posture and readiness. In the kicked-back action of sitting in an armchair, he was a coiled spring, ready to act in an instant's notice.

Daisy was actually a little nervous talking to him, which was weird for her. Usually she had no problem chatting with strangers. With him, though, she didn't want to say something wrong or sound like an idiot, and with her heart buzzing like it was, saying something wrong was a strong possibility.

She decided to continue with the security topic. "You have an immaculate suit. I can tell it's not off the rack. You're strong, but I can't tell if you've got Hulk muscles under there. You have this place memorized, and if the slightest thing changes in here you'll be the first to notice."

"Sounds like you've got me figured out." Even deep into the conversation, he still hardly looked at Daisy.

"My hang up is, you're not intimidating. No one is going to start something with any of us and look at you and think, *No way am I messing with that guy.* I just picture a bodyguard as someone with a seriously threatening demeanor."

There was that knowing grin again. He said, "That's probably good, since I'm best friends with a five-year old." The pride of that friendship shone on his face.

Her heart melted a little bit again. "It's your smile," she told him. "Who ever heard of a happy bodyguard? I mean, I can't imagine you carrying anything more dangerous than nail clippers." Even as she said it, she could feel the manliness pouring off of him. It was bugging her that she couldn't put her finger on it.

From across the aisle, Pasha called, "Your turn, Daisy Mae."

Cannon smirked, knowing he'd been saved from her prying. Daisy didn't want to go anywhere, but she forced herself to stand

and take Miss Dee's seat, wondering if maybe he was the kind of security guard who carried a cell phone to call for backup.

Nope, she knew instinctively that wasn't it. He probably did have a gun. That was probably his expertise. He was a gentleman body-guard, like James Bond. Suave and manly, but not built like a gorilla.

"Who won?" asked Daisy, feeling Cannon's eyes as they blipped over her.

"It was a draw," said Pasha with exasperation. "Again. That means it was a tie."

"Darn," said Daisy. "Do you want to go first?"

"Yes, thank you," said Pasha, picking up a red checker and drop-ping it into the middle slot. "We have to ... alternate next game. That means you go first."

Daisy dropped a black checker in without any type of strategy. She wasn't out for blood against a five-year old.

Cannon had stayed in the same chair, the one that gave him the best vantage of the parlour car while not allowing anyone to come up behind him. Miss Dee had taken the seat on the couch where Daisy had first sat. They both watched the game with interest, and suddenly Daisy felt like she was being hustled.

They alternated red and black checkers for a few turns and as Daisy picked up a black one to place it, she halted. There were two spots Pasha could get her, and Daisy could only block one. The game was as good as over and they'd only taken six turns each. Maybe Miss Dee really had learned Connect Four in college and then passed her knowledge on to Pasha.

Daisy slid her checker in and said, "You got me."

Pasha dropped in the red checker, connecting her four, and said, "I win. Good game. Play again?"

"Definitely," said Daisy. She was having fun with this brilliant little girl, even if she took Cannon out of the equation. Although, if she was being honest, what she wanted was some alone time with

Cannon to see if he would focus on her without his two little women distracting him.

"Sorry, Pasha," said Miss Dee. "It's time for your lesson."

The little girl scowled in disappointment but started picking up the pieces without being told. Daisy helped her and when they were done, Miss Dee and Cannon were standing in the aisle ready to go.

"Thank you for playing me," said Pasha. "It was fun to not draw *again*."

"Thank you for inviting me," said Daisy. She leaned down and whispered, loud enough for the adults to hear because she was grateful to them as well, "You kinda saved my train trip."

Pasha gave her a hug, and Daisy could see Cannon tense up. His eyes were locked on Daisy now, and Daisy knew for sure that Pasha was being body-guarded. She returned the quick hug, then stood, not wanting to make the guardians nervous.

"Miss Dee," said Pasha. "I want to ask you a private question, but I don't want to whisper in front of my new friend."

"I don't mind if you whisper or ask in front of me," said Daisy, "but thank you for being considerate."

Miss Dee gave a nod of agreement and waited for the question.

"May I invite Daisy Mae to dine with us this evening?"

The formality this little girl could put on was astonishing. She was like a little princess minus all the bratty attitude.

"Thank you so much for thinking of me," said Daisy, "but I brought food to eat." That seemed like the less embarrassing way to say she'd chosen the cheap fare to give the train a try and it didn't include meals.

"Of course she can," said Miss Dee. "We would be happy to have her as our guest if she will accept the invitation."

"I ..." She was about to say she couldn't, but Pasha was staring at her with those pleading eyes, and Miss Dee did seem sincere in the invitation. Daisy glanced at Cannon. Maybe he would give an indication of whether she would be intruding or not. He winked at her again!

Daisy tingled all over, feeling like a rock star had just noticed her. How could she turn down that wink? "I would love to. Thank you."

"We always get the six o'clock reservation," said Pasha. "We will meet you in the dining car when they make the announcement for the six o'clock people."

"What should I wear?" asked Daisy, taking advantage of her little guide while she had her.

"I always wear a dress. So does Miss Dee. Cannon wears a suit but he always wears a suit. Other people just wear normal clothes."

Daisy did love her fake boyfriend in a suit, but wouldn't mind seeing him in some other clothes eventually. For now, she was glad she'd made the last minute decision to bring a simple dress so she wouldn't be grossly underdressed. "That sounds lovely. I'll see you at six." She looked down at the seat and back at the door that led back to coach. "Pasha, do they care if I stay here in the parlour car all day?"

Pasha eagerly answered. "Any passenger can stay in the Pacific Parlour car, or the lounge car for as much time as they want. There's even a theater room downstairs from this car and they have movies and board games, but you gotta find someone to play with if you didn't bring someone."

All of those options sounded better than going back to her seat and Daisy breathed a sigh of relief. "I'm so glad to hear that."

"Any other questions," asked Pasha all full of hope.

"Not right now," said Daisy, "but I'm sure I'll have more by dinnertime."

"Bye, big sister."

"Bye, little sister."

Miss Dee led the way down the aisle and Pasha followed after.

Cannon paused in front of her, and Daisy hung on to what he

was about to say. Even if he didn't say anything, she'd be happy just standing here looking at him.

"Hang tight here for a second."

"Sure," said Daisy automatically, wondering if she could say no to her pretend boyfriend even if she tried.

Halfway up the car, Cannon halted his little trio in front of a nook of some sort, maybe it was a bar, and Cannon was talking to a train attendant. The attendant, a Hispanic man in a bowtie, nodded, and picked up a walkie talkie and spoke into it. A few seconds passed and he said something else into the walkie talkie, then exchanged a few words with Cannon.

They were talking about her. What did that mean?

As the trio started forward again, Cannon looked back to give Daisy a thumbs up and another little wink. She waved and tried to wink back, but it came out as a blink and a grimace.

Nice one, Daisy. Perfect image to leave him with. She watched with jealousy as the little family that wasn't made their way slowly to compensate for the light jolting of the train through the far door. There were still a few hours until dinner and those two lucky girls got to spend it with that happy, handsome man.

The attendant left his little enclosure and came toward her, breaking her trance.

"Miss Close?"

"Yes." Cannon had caught her last name. And remembered it. Daisy felt like she was in fifth grade and her crush had just said, *Hi, Daisy* to her on the playground.

"I'm Felix. I understand you ended up with an ... unfortunate seating arrangement."

"Yeah. I mean, it's not ..." She was going to say it wasn't a big deal, but it actually was a big deal. "Can you change my seat?" Some unlucky person in coach would be disappointed to have someone take the empty spot next to them, but at least Daisy had had the luxury of a shower today so she wouldn't be too bad to sit by.

"I can do better than that," said Felix. "I can either upgrade you to Business Select, or put you in a roomette."

"Really? Wow. That would be incredible."

"Which one sounds better?" asked Felix. "Do you know the difference between those options?"

Daisy knew very well since she'd examined in depth the options before booking her ticket. "I'd love a roomette," she said.

"If you want to grab your items, I'll show you to your roomette. You can find me right over there."

"Thank you," said Daisy, but she knew she should be thanking Cannon. Wow, her guardian angel had let her down originally, but was making up for it big time. Cannon was turning out to be a perfect fantasy boyfriend.

2

Cannon was counting the minutes until six o'clock. He'd been doing this run with Pasha and Miss Dee for over a year, every week without fail, and he'd never looked forward to dinner more than he did tonight. When Rasmus Gold, Pasha's father, had hired him—through Sutton Smith's Warrior Project—to escort his daughter between his home in Seattle and Pasha's mother's home in Los Angeles, Rasmus had told Pasha that if anything went wrong on the train, she should run to Cannon. He hadn't used the word bodyguard with Pasha. Kneeling and looking into his daughter's eyes, Rasmus had said, *Cannon is your new best friend.*

Not a bad job title, especially for a kid as great as Pasha, but today, after his best friend had picked the prettiest girl in California to be their companion on this trip, she really was his best friend. If Cannon wasn't working, he'd be spending the rest of this trip going after Daisy like a heat-seeking missile. Daisy Mae Close. He hadn't been able to get her pretty face out of his head since he'd escorted Pasha and Miss Dee back to their car for her tutoring.

She had such a pure, girl-next-door look to her and it seemed so genuine. Even her blonde hair looked natural, not dyed. Living in Southern California, it seemed that everywhere he went, the women were more plastic than human. Unlike Miss Dee, who was as cultured as they came, and dignified enough that it wouldn't surprise Cannon if she married British royalty, Daisy seemed so real and fun and down-to-earth. She was so easy to talk to and banter with, and that was just in the few moments he'd had with her so far. And to top it all off, she was so effortlessly ... kind.

When the guy next to her in coach started coughing up a lung, she offered what she could to help instead of trying to hide from Mr. Communicable. And the way she engaged so thoroughly with a five-year-old stranger when she surely had better things to do on the train.

That wasn't all, though. Daisy had something about her, a good-ness that he found irresistible. She was everything he'd been trying to attract in his life ever since he left the SEALs. In Daisy's presence, the darkness of the world and of his past life had no power or influ-ence on him, as if the ground she walked on was sacred ground and everyone in her presence benefited from some sort of halo effect.

And to think she was just across the hallway. Cannon had been resisting the urge to tap on the door to see if she wanted to chat, or to point out some landmarks as they passed them. Anything to be near her. But for now his focus had to be on his job, his duty to protect Pasha.

After the Connect Four matches, Miss Dee and Pasha had made a detour to the café below the lounge car so Pasha could get her accus-tomed snack. By the time they'd made it to their rooms, Daisy had already arrived in the normally empty sleeper and had the curtains pulled and door closed. At least Daisy was on the scenic side of the train —if she hadn't been, he would have switched rooms with her. The views of the Pacific Ocean as they traveled up the coast were unparalleled.

Pasha and Miss Dee always stayed in the same car on these trips —a bottom-floor bedroom suite at the front of the car. Unlike most of the rooms, which had an aisle going past them, there was only one way in and one way out of their suite. Cannon always had the same room, as well, the roomette next door. It was just the right size for one person, but it was designed for two people, as long as they liked each other a lot. It was basically two bench seats facing each other, and not a whole lot else. The room across the walkway from Cannon was usually empty, an extra buffer and a room Cannon could set up in if he wanted a slightly different vantage point of the hall approaching Pasha's suite.

From Cannon's lookout spot on his seat, he could see up the hallway, making it impossible for anyone to gain access to Pasha's room without him seeing them. For the 36-hours of the trip, Cannon would stay awake, constantly vigilant for any threat to his little charge.

Rasmus was an international celebrity, entrepreneur, and pioneer of green energy, and had received various threats against himself and his family. Sutton and Cannon had discussed the specific threats at length, and while they seemed like the kind of drivel any big celebrity would receive, Rasmus was nervous enough that Big Oil, or Big Electric, or Big Any-Other-Standard-Energy would try to stop his public momentum, that he was taking no risks with his only daughter's safety. His wealth alone made Pasha's kidnapping a possibility.

When Rasmus Gold hired him through Sutton Smith, he insisted on finding one man, and one man only, to keep his daughter safe on the frequent trips. He loved the idea of a former SEAL. *If he can survive Hell Week*, Rasmus had said, *he can stay alert for 36 hours on a train.* However, he was concerned that someone skilled enough and ruthless enough to stop any sort of threat with extreme force wouldn't be a good influence around his daughter. He had almost given up when he'd come across Sutton Smith's unique organization.

Rasmus had personally met all of Sutton's SEALs and chosen Cannon for two reasons: his kid-friendly personality and the dozen or so weapons and self-defense gadgets he carried hidden on his person.

Sutton and Cannon had had some fun at the other former SEALs' expense when Sutton had told them all of Rasmus Gold's impression of the other guys. Corbin had lost his temper in the interview when Rasmus baited him by saying snipers were sissies and cowards. Rasmus didn't like the way Blayze had tried to do a Sherlock-thing, reading him like some deductive psychoanalyst. Running in elite circles, Rasmus knew River Duncan's family and said he didn't trust a rich kid to be ruthless enough if things went south. But the best was Zane. Rasmus had passed him up because he looked too much like Thor.

Not to be outdone, the guys had started calling Cannon Barney the Babysitter.

Cannon could understand Rasmus Gold's concern. Cannon wasn't even Pasha's father, but he loved that little girl. With all the bad things in the world, he needed something like this bright little girl to help him stay on the sunny side of life. If things ever did go wrong, he'd give his life protecting her without a second thought. Though the more likely case was him sending anyone who threatened Pasha to meet his Maker.

Someday he'd have someone special like that in his own life. A wife, a daughter. Something was missing in his life for sure.

Cannon's eyes went to the door of the room across from his. A woman like Daisy would change everything. The peace and the light he craved so badly seemed to be embodied in her. Daisy Mae. He couldn't wait to get to know her better, but that was so hard under the circumstances. For now all he could do was try to stay focused.

If he wasn't so hyper-vigilant, he might think Daisy had closed up the room and gone back to one of the viewing cars, but watching as intently as he was, he could tell by a slight shadow under the door, and faint sounds of movement, that she was in there.

"A long, long time ago..."

Cannon sat up and looked around. Someone was singing.

"... I can still remember ... how the music used to make me smile."

It was Daisy! She wasn't belting it out, just singing like there was a song in her that wanted to come out, so she sang. Cannon stood carefully, not wanting to draw any attention, and stepped into the aisle. "American Pie" was usually nostalgic and almost mournful, but from Daisy's lips it was sweet and pure.

Cannon was enthralled and realized he'd been drawn to it like a siren's call at the expense of everything else around him. He shook his head and turned to watch down the hallway, but kept his ears peeled to the angel singing on the other side of the roomette door. Daisy's was the sweetest voice he'd ever heard, and the suddenness and nearness of her pleasing tone made him feel like he'd come home after a long journey.

Cannon loved his job and always appreciated it, but he'd never enjoyed it nearly as much as right in this very moment. If he could listen to her sing on every trip, he'd do the job for free.

The overhead speaker went off, making Cannon jump. Gustav announced dinner for people with the six o'clock reservation.

The singing stopped immediately. Cannon had never been so frustrated by any of the train employees. He reached into his pocket and pulled out his handkerchief to wipe his eyes.

Daisy's door opened, and there she stood in a light dress with short flowy sleeves. It had a blue flower pattern on it that set off her eyes like bluebells. He wanted to call it a summer dress, but he wasn't sure that was the actual name of it, but it was so Daisy. It didn't matter how you described it, she was stunning.

She startled when she saw him. "Oh, I didn't know we were neighbors."

"There goes the neighborhood," he said.

Shoot! This wasn't one of his SEAL buddies who he could banter with. The Navy needed to start offering classes on how to talk to girls when guys left the Navy because after ten years of service, it was hard to break the tough-brother banter, even after being out for over a year.

She smiled, apparently unsure how to respond.

"You look nice," he said.

"Thanks," said Daisy. In a playful tone she added, "I'd tell you that you look nice, but apparently it's how you always look."

Oh good. If she was still bantering with him, he wasn't doing too bad. He smiled back at her hoping it wasn't too obvious he'd been so touched by her singing.

"Should I wait?" asked Daisy.

"Nah," said Cannon quietly. "Pasha would prefer meeting you in the dining car." Daisy had to know where it was because you had to go through it to get from the parlour car to the sleeper.

"See you there," said Daisy, giving him that perfect hometown smile. The center of her left cheek dimpled into a dot and Cannon had to concentrate to keep his smile from taking over his whole face.

"See you there."

He watched her disappear around the corner of the stairwell, unable to ignore the feeling that he needed her in his life. He'd never fallen for someone this quickly before, and didn't know what to do with the electricity running through his veins.

The door behind him opened, and Pasha stepped through wearing a sleeveless pink dress and a matching bow in her hair.

"You look lovely this evening, Miss Pasha," said Cannon.

"Thank you," said Pasha. "You look handsome, even though it's the same as you always look."

He smiled at her response noting how similar it was to his other favorite girl on the train. "Shall we?" he asked. Cannon wanted to offer her an arm and escort her through the cars but the passageways were too narrow, not to mention it was logistically impossible to do proper security from such a posture.

Their passage through the cars was a choreographed routine so Cannon could keep an eye on Pasha from behind and also clear each car before she went in. Pasha always stayed in the middle while the adults traded places.

When they walked into the dining car, Daisy was standing there in the back of a line of five people. Gustav, the dining car attendant, seated the other four at a table in the center of the car.

Daisy was watching him and Miss Dee, ready to follow their lead.

"This is our table," said Pasha, pointing at the table to their left. "But we hafta wait till Gustav sits us. That's one of the manners of the dining car."

"Thanks," said Daisy.

Cannon could see her glance at all the empty tables between them and the rest of the diners, trying to figure out why they got special treatment.

Once Gustav had seated the other four, he walked up to their group, smiling. "How is my little poet?" he asked Pasha.

"I'm not a poet," she replied. "I don't write poems, I just learn them and say them."

"I hope you have one for me tonight," he said. "After dessert?"

"It would be my pleasure," said Pasha.

Gustav bowed, then motioned them to take seats in the table Pasha had already pointed out. Pasha and Daisy took the inside seats, with Cannon taking the seat next to Pasha that gave him his back to the wall and a clear view of the entire car. Not to mention a great view of Daisy every time his eyes went to the view outside of the window.

Just as he had earlier, Cannon had to focus to keep his eyes on everything in the car and not focused on Daisy. However, he did notice every move she made as he noticed everything in the car. The difference was, when she smiled, he felt like the sun had risen in the dining car.

Pasha wouldn't mind if he flirted—she'd probably encourage it —but he had a duty to perform, and if Daisy became too much of a distraction, he would take steps to separate her from them.

Steps to separate her from them? Wow, that sounded way more like a violent SEAL mission than he'd intended.

Seeing Daisy and Miss Dee sitting side by side—Daisy's natural beauty, easy smile, and inner brightness and Miss Dee's poised demeanor, professional level makeup, and lustrous dark hair that perfectly matched her brown eyes—there was no doubt Cannon preferred Daisy's style. He couldn't really put a finger on it; it was just something positive and wholesome he felt around her.

He saw her eyes grow momentarily wide when she noticed the prices on the menu.

Whether Pasha had noticed or whether she was just being a good host, she said, "You can get whatever you want. Everything is included already. It's covered."

They occasionally had guests dine with them on the train and Miss Dee had trained Pasha in putting their guests at ease. Most people already knew that about the meals, but some of them were new to the train, or had been in coach, like Daisy, and weren't sure.

As she had in the parlour car, Daisy did a quick eye-check with Cannon and he gave her another little nod to confirm.

To Pasha, she said, "Well aren't you the most gracious little hostess?"

Cannon saw Pasha blush under the praise. She said, "We ride the train every week and I make a lot of friends."

Gustav arrived and took drink orders. The adults ordered water and the young lady ordered apple juice. Cannon would save the caffeine intake for later tonight.

There were two servers who covered the dining car, but Gustav, who ran the dining car, always saw to Pasha and her group himself. He'd been background-checked by Rasmus Gold's staff and received some basic training on what to look for in order to prevent any sort of poisoning attempt. No one but the cooks and Gustav handled the food for Miss Pasha and her escorts.

"What's good?" Daisy asked Pasha.

"Well I like the macaroni and cheese. You're allowed to order it, even though it's on the kids menu."

Daisy looked as if she was considering it, but Cannon was certain she wouldn't order the seven-dollar mac and cheese when there was salmon, steak, and Surf and Turf on the menu. Gustav brought their drinks and took their orders. As planned, Pasha got the mac and cheese. The ladies both went with the salmon and Cannon got the steak.

Pasha showed Daisy how to lay out her silverware, then started her standard interview questions. Cannon had been through this interview process at least a dozen times. Pasha's parents wanted her to have well-rounded social skills, and the little prodigy was already a better conversationalist at five-years old than Cannon was at twenty-nine.

Cannon listened with interest, wanting to ask follow-up questions and get answers of his own, but he let his little spy do all the digging. Everything Daisy did affected him. Her laugh, the way she pushed her blonde hair behind her ear, and just her bright ... countenance made him feel all energetic and optimistic, like everything was going to be all right forever.

Am I in love or something? he wondered. Was that possible? They'd just barely met.

"What do you do, Daisy? For a living?" asked Pasha

"I'm a freelance book editor," said Daisy. Pasha had stalled and it was obvious by the look on her face that didn't ring a bell. "When people write books, they need someone to read it and make sure it's a really good book and that there aren't a lot of mistakes."

A book lover too? If he hadn't been in love before, that might just push him over the edge. "Reading books for a living," said Cannon, venturing boldly into the conversation. "Not too shabby."

Cannon wanted to find out what kind of books, and find out if he'd ever read any of them. But he was afraid if he started talking too much, it would too easily become a two-person conversation. It could also be a distraction to him from his job so he closed his mouth and his little best friend did the dirty work for him.

"Almost as nice as riding a train for a living," countered Daisy.

Pasha covered her mouth with the back of her hand and in whisper they could all hear, said, "I think you just got burned."

Cannon couldn't argue with that and he chuckled along with Daisy. Miss Dee was close to laughing, and Cannon wondered if she would correct Pasha's playful impertinence. She ended up letting it pass.

Daisy added, "It's not my job, but I volunteer at the Christmas House. That's a place that helps kids who don't have a home of their own."

Now Cannon knew he'd found his soul mate. He just had to figure out how to let Daisy know.

Dinner and dessert went along the same track with Pasha tirelessly interviewing Daisy and finding out everything about this woman. Well, a small fraction of everything, since Cannon just wanted to know more and more. The food was delicious, as usual, and Daisy seemed to have no problem rolling with the formalities of the table. A year ago, Cannon had needed in-depth lessons on etiquette since he was expected to model the behavior Pasha's parents wanted her to learn.

After their dessert plates were cleared off, Gustav appeared. "Are you ready to recite your poem, Miss Pasha?"

"Yes I am. It's kinda a scary one, but also kinda fun." She cleared her throat, then her eyes got all intense. "'Jabberwocky', by Lewis Carroll. Twas brillig and the slithy toves did gyre and gimble in the wabe."

Pasha knew the entire poem and performed it as if she'd been practicing for months. When she said, "... snicker snack," with her cute little lisp, it was the cutest thing ever.

When she finished, the four adults clapped and Daisy said, "Snicker-snack!" Pasha smiled and chair-curtsied a couple of times, and Gustav thanked her and left.

Miss Dee said in her formal British accent, "I'm sure Daisy is exhausted from all of the questions."

Without being prompted, Pasha said, "Thank you for dining with us, Daisy."

"It was my pleasure," said Daisy. "Now that we're neighbors I'm sure we can play Connect Four tomorrow. Plus," she said, winking at Cannon, but talking to Pasha, "I can give you some tips for dealing with loud neighbors on the train who throw crazy parties."

"We're neighbors?" Pasha missed entirely the joke intended for Cannon. "Yay! Okay, I'll come over after breakfast. This time I'll give you some pointers before we play so you can do better."

They all stood from the table and Miss Dee left a large tip for Gustav. That had taken some getting used to—Miss Dee covering every expense. It had been months since he'd balked at it, but having Daisy here witnessing their dynamics made him self-conscious about things like that. Cannon brushed it off, thinking about what a great life he had, and they started in to their normal routine to make it back to their sleeper.

Having Daisy in the mix confused the choreography, even though she did nothing other than stay in the back of the group the whole time. Cannon was used to their routine and it didn't involve keeping an eye on someone who was still kind of a stranger or holding doors open for her as they went from car to car.

"Let's wait here for a sec, Pash. Let Daisy go ahead so we don't slow her down."

She must have picked up on his discomfort because she didn't argue, saying, "See ya later, little sis," as she passed. When Cannon's procession made it to their rooms, Daisy was coming out of her room, holding a toothbrush. She stepped in to one of the common restrooms.

Pasha and Miss Dee went into their suite to put pajamas on and Cannon got really casual by loosening his tie. He didn't mind the suit one bit. Compared to the fatigues and gear he'd worn in the Philippines, Somalia, and in the Middle East, this was like wearing sweats. Plus, it gave him places to hide guns and gadgets.

Without really planning to, Cannon stepped into Daisy's room and peeked in her purse. She had a small mace canister, but no other weapons. Snooping was not a cool thing to do, but his priority was Pasha and they'd brought Daisy right up close and personal. He needed to have some peace of mind about her. He knew his priorities while he was guarding his sweet little best friend. If someone *was* trying to hurt her, getting close by becoming a friend or sister would be a genius way to do it.

Hoping Daisy would take a minute, he lifted the flap of her carry-on and did a quick assessment of the contents. Clothes, including intimates that made him blush, some books, charging cords. No weapons, bombs, spy equipment, poisons. She seemed to be on the up and up. Leaving everything exactly as he'd found it, he stepped out and backed into his own room.

No sooner had he cleared the threshold of his room, than the restroom door opened and Daisy came out.

"Goodnight," said Daisy as she stepped into her room.

"Goodnight," he answered automatically, but was embarrassed, so he added, "John-boy." Goodnight sounded so intimate. Since high school, he'd only ever said goodnight to Pasha. Well maybe his

SEAL buddies but only if it was accompanied by something like, *"Goodnight, you filthy animals."*

She looked at him funny, obviously not following.

"The Waltons?" he explained. "Old TV show?"

Daisy shook her head, and he felt even stupider. Why was he failing so hard with simple banter?

"Goodnight," he said simply, feeling the red rise on his cheeks.

She pulled her door closed, then the curtains.

Cannon face-palmed and breathed a sigh of relief. Daisy was great to be around, but having her near definitely didn't make his job any easier. Did he regret bringing her close? It wouldn't make the night easy knowing she was right on the other side of the sliding door, just a light knock away, and he felt like he'd been doing his job by asking Felix to set her up in that room. Not only had it been excellent socialization for Pasha, but Miss Dee would take the opportunity to point out Daisy's sticky situation and highlight the kindness they'd done for their new friend.

He still had about 24 hours of being near enough to Daisy to reach out and touch her. Did she need help figuring out how to transform the seats into a bed? And would she know that the bedding was on top of the upper bunk?

She could figure it out. There were printed instructions in her roomette, and she obviously knew how to read, since she was a book editor.

The door to Pasha's suite opened, saving him from more agonizing over the irresistible train companion. "Hey, Pash." She was wearing her Moana PJs so he already knew what movie was on the schedule. "What movie do you want to watch tonight?" As if that wasn't enough of a hint, Miss Dee was holding the *Moana* Blu-Ray.

Pasha gave him a disbelieving look. "Can't you guess? There are clues all around."

"Hm," said Cannon. "We're on a train, so maybe it's *Thomas and Friends.*"

"Nope."

The curtain to Daisy's room twitched, and he saw one gorgeous blue eyeball peeking out.

For half a second, Cannon paused, not wanting to leave Daisy but he caught himself and started leading the group down the corridor and up the stairs, revolving around Pasha as they went. "There's a train in *Planes Fire and Rescue*."

"It doesn't have anything with trains," said Pasha.

"No trains? Ok, is it *Toy Story 3*? There are no trains in *Toy Story 3*."

"Yes, Cannon. There's a train robbing scene with Mr. Potato Head. He's One Eye Bart, remember?"

"That's right," said Cannon. "*Dumbo*?"

"Circus train," said Pasha.

"*Zootopia*?"

"Train."

"*Lady and the Tramp*?"

"Train."

With fake exasperation, Cannon said, "What movies don't have trains?"

"You're just trying'a get me to tell you the answer."

That strategy had worked before, but she was on to him. "Okay, so there are clues all around. Hmmm."

Pasha stopped at the next door and spread her arms to show off her pajamas. "Any ideas?"

"Let's see," said Cannon. "Beautiful girl, blonde hair, pajamas ... I know! *Sleeping Beauty*."

She giggled. "No, Cannon. Look closer." She pointed right at the picture of Moana on her PJ top.

"I got it! *Moana*!"

"Phew," said Pasha, holding up a hand to give him a high five. "I thought you wouldn't get it until the movie was already over." They reached the parlour car and took the stairs down to the theater room. Miss Dee set up the movie while Cannon took his place by the aisle in the last row of the theater-style seats at the back of the room.

He'd seen Moana about a dozen times. Well, he'd been in the room while Moana played about a dozen times. This time, as he kept one eye on the door at the back of the room and one eye on the rest of the room, he hoped the door would open and in would walk a sweet, blonde beauty. If he would have been thinking, he would have suggested Pasha invite her. Instead he was left with a smile on his face and plans to ask her out when they got off the train in Seattle tomorrow night.

3

Daisy woke up, in a dark room, lying on a bed that was not her own. The room was ... trembling.

Oh, the train. She'd been up late editing, and since she'd already brushed her teeth, she hadn't bothered getting up to go to the bathroom when her eyelids started to close. Her phone said it was 3:30. She wouldn't make it until morning. Not with the train jostling like that.

There was barely room to stand in the tiny room. As soon as she got her feet under her, she slid her door open and shuffled out into the hallway. Cannon's room was dark, but his door was open. So either he was out patrolling or he just slept with his door open. She turned toward the restroom.

"Boo," said a voice from Cannon's room.

"Ee!" said Daisy, spinning and clutching her chest.

Cannon chuckled as he leaned out into the light.

"Are you crazy?" she whispered. "Startling someone with a full bladder!"

"It's okay," he said. "I know where they keep the mops." He

immediately grimaced and shook his head. "Sorry. That probably wasn't appropriate."

"It's true," she said, wishing she was the one in the dark so he couldn't see what she looked like. "I'll be right back." She turned back toward the bathroom and hurried in. Yeah, she looked like she'd slept in a clothes dryer. And there he'd been all GQ in his black suit. Did he just sit there awake all night?

She could only stay in the bathroom so long, and there was only so much she could do without a brush or any makeup. Not that she wore very much, but anything would help at this hour of the night. Suddenly she wasn't sleepy at all. Maybe he'd be up for a late-night conversation. She could dream, right? It was worth a shot of getting some one-on-one time with him to risk being seen in her present state.

When Daisy went back into the hallway, Cannon was gone. Approaching more slowly, she didn't jump or scream this time when his head and shoulders emerged into the dim light.

"What are you doing up," she asked quietly, leaning against the frame of her doorway, hoping she was at least partially in the shadows of her room.

"Reading," he said.

"What book? Maybe I edited it."

He got that amused smile on his face. "I doubt it."

"Try me," she said, loving the playful way he smiled like that and really curious now.

He held up a small Bible, and she imagined it tucked in a soldier's pocket, saving his life when it caught a bullet for him.

"What part are you reading?"

Cannon looked down at it and his eyes lost focus. It seemed like he was trying to decide how much to tell her. Without looking up he said, "You know the woman who touches Jesus's robe and is healed? That one."

For whatever reason, she could tell it was special to him. She stepped forward and knelt to his level. "Why that one?"

He was still zoned out, which gave her hope that he might open up. "I just wonder if she ever, you know, wondered if she was worthy to do that. It was just the hem of his robe, but ..." he shrugged.

Daisy wanted to go into his roomette, squeeze onto the seat next to him and put an arm around him. But he was so vulnerable and open, she didn't want to move and break the spell.

"What do you think?" he asked, bringing his eyes up to meet hers.

I think you are the most gorgeous, strong, sensitive man on the planet. Somehow she refrained from telling him that. Instead, she reached a hand up to his face and rested it on his cheek. His five-o'clock shadow was rough, and she could feel the hard muscles of his jaw. Maybe he'd kiss her. She looked at his lips and suddenly her mouth was salivating.

Cannon sighed and closed his eyes, but only for a split second. Clearing his throat, he stood slowly, bringing her up with him. "You, uh, you don't have to kneel in the hallway. Why don't you sit in your roomette?"

Her heart crashed a little at losing the physical contact, but Daisy remembered how horrible she looked and backed into her room and took a seat. That moment had been so tender and memorable, but it was past now. If she wanted to get it back she'd have to ease into it.

Cannon leaned into her room and put a finger on the nightlight switch. "Do you mind if I turn this on? I really want to be able to see you."

Daisy studied him for a moment, taking her time because he was still right there, close enough to reach out and touch. Close enough to pick up that light cologne that reminded her of leather. "Is that a professional question or personal?"

Cannon studied her right back, only inches away, giving her nice tingles up and down her arms.

"Both."

That wasn't the exact answer she was looking for, but it still made her happy that he was admitting it was at least partially personal so she nodded and he clicked the light.

"Why do you ride the train?" she asked as he stepped back into the hallway, leaning against her door, with his back to Pasha's door. "Wouldn't flying be faster? Cheaper?"

Again, he considered. Slowly he said, "Pasha loves riding the train, and daddy can't tell her no."

"Job security for you, I guess," she said.

Cannon chuckled. "That's right."

"So you watched *Moana*?"

"You were peeking at us," he replied. "I saw you."

"You're so great with her," said Daisy. "Do you have kids of your own?" If she was going to get the details on her midnight boyfriend she might as well be bold.

"No. You?"

"No. Never been married." Engaged, though. Was now the time to tell him? No way.

"But you got plenty of kids at the Christmas Box House."

"Yeah," she said, smiling at the thought of those beautiful, unlucky kiddos. "I've had so many blessings in my life. I feel so blessed and I want to share some of that."

Cannon was nodding slowly. That was kind of the opposite of his reasoning. He'd been through the pain a lot of the kids suffered and wanted to end it. "They need it. I do a little bit of work with the kids at my church. I want to get more involved."

"That's awesome," said Daisy. Her heart was overflowing with love and respect for this man. "What's keeping you from doing it?"

"It's not ... you can't just get a job doing it, get trained and go do it. I feel like a ministry like that takes some more time to be ... *ready* for."

The way he said 'ready' made her wonder what he really meant, so she asked him. "What do you mean?"

"Nothing," he said, standing a little more at attention. "Just a sec."

She expected him to walk away for a minute, but he stayed in place. After a few seconds she heard soft footsteps in the hallway and the restroom door open then close. Since Cannon kept staring intently ahead, Daisy stayed quiet. After a minute, she heard the door again and someone walking away.

"What were we talking about?" asked Cannon.

She suspected he was dodging her previous question, but she wasn't going to push it. "Kids. No wonder you are a bodyguard for a little girl, but who in the world would want to hurt a little angel like her?"

Cannon studied her like he didn't understand the question. Daisy knew she was naïve sometimes, but really she couldn't imagine any real life person wanting to hurt Pasha.

"That's what makes you so ..." He thought for a long time before he finally said, "Alluring."

Ooh, that was good. Daisy suppressed her silly smile. She felt an overwhelming urge to sing.

"You edit novels, right? Isn't there violence in your books?"

"Yeah," she said, "but that's fiction. It's not real life."

He raised one eyebrow and just looked at her almost as if he were waiting for her to catch up.

"So there really are people out there who would hurt that little angel?" The thought made her heart hurt.

"Unfortunately," said Cannon, looking out the window into the night. "There's a lot of darkness in the world. Where I grew up in Oakland, and in the military, I saw so much of it." He exhaled, thinking for a minute, then said. "Sometimes I wonder how much has stuck to me."

Daisy was about to tell him there was nothing dark about him from what she could see, but he looked at her so ... adoringly and said, "Then I see you and I just feel like the world is filled with light. I don't know what your life's been like, but nothing bad or dark has ever stuck to you."

She felt like their souls were connecting. Yeah, she'd lived a sheltered life and avoided a lot of the bad things she read about in books and saw in the media. She'd basically convinced herself that it was all made up and only existed in fiction. To hear him say that she didn't have any darkness attached to her was one of the sweetest things he could possibly say. It broke her heart what he said about himself, though.

"I don't see darkness in you," she told him. "I can tell you have some ... turbulence, but you don't let it show."

They stared at each other for a while, not even needing words to communicate. On an unseen cue, Cannon snapped to attention and watched the hallway. She heard someone scuffing their feet, then the bathroom door opened and closed.

A part of her was glad to be free of the intense spell of his eyes, but deep down, she just wanted more of this amazing man.

When the bathroom visitor finished and returned to their cabin, Daisy said, "I want to know more about you. About the controlled havoc deep down in there." She reached forward and touched his chest lightly. His very muscular chest.

Cannon just breathed for a minute, staring blankly down the hallway. "You can't walk through mud without it sticking to you. I've been through a lot of mud. I try to keep it all jammed down inside where it can't affect my life, but it's still there."

Suddenly his gaze snapped up to her face, and she jolted at the sharpness of it, all the while loving his penetrating emerald eyes.

"Things are different around you, Daisy. The darkness isn't there. All I can see is light and goodness."

Daisy had never wanted to kiss someone so badly in her life, and she found herself staring at his well-formed lips.

Cannon snapped to attention, and a few seconds later she picked up the sounds of someone in the hallway again. It gave her a minute to catch her breath.

When the coast was clear again, he said, "I don't know why all of that just spilled out. You're gonna think I'm crazy and that I'm going to start saying I can't live without you or something." He gave her that knee-weakening amused smile again. "I promise I'm not psycho."

Daisy didn't even have to talk. She could sit here all night, just listening to him. However, she didn't want him to think she was some kind of stalker or weirdo so she said, "I should turn in."

"Yeah," he said. "Thanks for being my therapist. Send me a bill, huh?"

Daisy laughed lightly. "See you in a few hours." She slid her door closed.

She didn't just want more of Cannon. She wanted much, much more.

4

Daisy stayed in her roomette until the first call for breakfast was made around seven a.m. She didn't know if she was expected to dine with her new sister and fake boyfriend or if she was on her own for today. It had been less than two hours since she'd gone to sleep but the thought of seeing him again had her up and energized.

There were the plans for Connect Four, but they hadn't made plans beyond that. Daisy didn't even know if the rest of her meals were covered or not, since she was a coach passenger riding in a roomette. Better play it safe and just eat the granola bars and trail mix she'd brought with her.

She pulled back her curtain and slid her door open and there was Cannon, looking up at her from his seat in the roomette across the hall. Without thinking, Daisy stepped back and pulled her curtain shut, then stood there with her heart racing. The door was still open, and she couldn't shut it without opening the curtain again.

"I can see you," he said, chuckling.

Daisy looked down and realized her legs and feet were clearly visible below the curtain. How did she get out of this one? And why wasn't she expecting him to be there! If he wasn't so dang perfect, she wouldn't be so off her game. The window popped out in an emergency, right? How badly would she get hurt if she jumped out at 60 miles per hour?

"Come on out," said Cannon.

Daisy was stuck. Now she couldn't even take a minute to get presentable. She picked up her toiletry bag and slid the curtain back. She completely forgot about herself when she saw him as perfect as yesterday with his immaculate suit, perfect brown hair, and sparkling green eyes. And had he shaved sometime during the night? Unlike Daisy, who hadn't even thought about doing anything with her hair and still wore the sweatpants and t-shirt she'd slept in, he looked ready to dine with the president. At least Daisy had thought to put a bra on. That was something at least.

Remembering her predicament made her start sweating.

"Morning," he said.

"Did you sleep okay?" she asked sliding past and inching toward the bathroom. Even at the crack of dawn, he still wore that smile like it was great living in his world.

"Nope. Thank goodness."

"Oh, that's right." Duh, he stayed awake all night. "I'm just gonna ..." She escaped down the hall and into the bathroom.

The tiny bathroom felt claustrophobic. Daisy's pulse was racing like she'd run a mile. To make matters worse, in the small mirror of the restroom, she saw a train wreck looking back at her. Her hair was going every direction, and her face was still puffy from sleep. She'd stayed up talking to him way too late last night, and the bags under her eyes showed it. Makeup wasn't a huge part of her life, but she did put on moisturizer, as well as a little eye shadow and mascara. Without it, and so early in the morning, she looked pasty and puffy. Hopefully Cannon liked glazed donuts because that's what she'd looked like out in the hallway.

Not that he'd seemed to mind. Not late last night and not just now. His bright face had brightened even more when she came out of her room and started chatting.

Daisy did what she could with her hair and brushed her teeth. When she went back out, Cannon was in his same spot keeping an eye on everything. He smiled at her when they made eye contact, and it made Daisy feel like Cinderella.

Walking down the corridor in my dirty servant's clothes I approached the prince's quarters. Our eyes met and I froze, trapped in the spell of his emerald eyes. The world around me shimmered and I looked down to see my clothes had been transformed to a deep blue embroidered ball gown. My ratty hair was up in a princess-do complete with a jeweled tiara. In an instant I had become the most beautiful lady in the kingdom.

"Are you okay?" asked Cannon. He was standing and reaching out a hand to her.

Oh perfect. She had been gazing at him all dream-like. Dang him and that enchanting smile. "Sorry, I was lost in the sway of the train for a second."

"Wait, you were, what was it I said yesterday? Mind switching?"

The door at the end of the hallway opened and out stepped Miss Dee—looking as perfect as the night before, but not as perfect as Cannon's smile had made Daisy feel—followed by Pasha, wearing a pair of designer jeans, tan blouse, and a Supreme brand hoodie.

"Good morning," said Daisy, happy for the rescue.

Pasha ran past Miss Dee and gave Daisy a hug. "Hi, Daisy Mae. I have to eat breakfast before we can play Connect Four."

"That's fine," said Daisy.

"You're coming with us, right, big sister? To breakfast?"

"Yes, please do," said Miss Dee.

Daisy checked with Cannon and got a tiny nod. Unfortunately no wink this time, but that did make three invitations. "Of course," said Daisy. "Can I meet you there in a few minutes? I don't want to wear my PJs to the dining car."

"Yeah that's okay," said Pasha. "Even though I'd wear PJs all day if I was allowed." She looked up at Miss Dee, who shook her head and tried to suppress a smile at the absurd idea.

"Save me a seat, okay, sis?" said Daisy.

"You got it," said Pasha, and the three of them did the little dance they did when they went through the corridors, changing places at every junction, which made it kind of hard to track him all the way.

At breakfast, instead of watching the scenery go by, they got to look at the train station in the town of Klamath Falls, Oregon. There would be an hour delay due to conductor staffing issues. Daisy didn't care—she was on a train, and who rode a train if they were in a hurry? Besides, the company wasn't bad at all, especially the late night company. And if they got sick of her, Daisy had plenty of work to do.

After breakfast they went back to the parlour car and Pasha beat Daisy in four straight games of Connect Four. The trio excused themselves for tutoring sessions and Daisy envisioned that Pasha might just be the mental equivalent of a high school senior by the time she started first grade. Daisy grabbed her laptop, took it to the lounge car, and spent the next couple of hours editing as the majestic forests of Oregon rolled past her window. It was a colossal sea of trees that seemed as vast as the oceans.

The four of them ate lunch together, played Mancala—which Daisy managed to win two out of like eight games—then after her afternoon tutoring, dinner. As much as Daisy enjoyed spending time with the brilliant little Pasha, it was Cannon whom she longed to see. Unfortunately, he had barely said two words to her after Pasha and Miss Dee had appeared that morning. Around them he was all business, and Daisy was all but forgotten.

She'd never been so torn about a man. Even with Sterling, she liked him enough to spend years with him. Throughout his medical residency she'd always assumed that when that life was over, she would take a more prominent role, but life hadn't changed when he became a real doctor. Daisy was still less important than his career and she had felt it nearly every day. Less than a week before the wedding, a friend of his had insulted her, and instead of defending her, Sterling laughed it off. Daisy called off the engagement then and there.

And here she was falling all over again for a guy who only noticed her because he noticed everything in the room. Except when they were alone, of course, but hadn't Sterling been like that? It was when any sort of distraction came up that she was pushed to the side. The problem was, all the feelings she'd ever felt for Sterling didn't compare to how drawn she was to Cannon. He was like a walking, talking fantasy for her, minus the talking part for most of the day. Maybe it was his reticence that drew her to him. Maybe if he all of a sudden took an interest in her it would remove the mystery and she'd be put off. She sincerely doubted it, but maybe.

As the train approached Seattle, Daisy packed up her things. The sliding door to her roomette was open, as was Cannon's, but he was too busy staring down the empty aisle to notice her. A voice over the intercom announced their arrival and thanked them for riding with Amtrak.

She and Cannon stepped up to their doorways at the same time. Before she could be whisked away into a fantasy, he said her name.

"Daisy?"

Heart fluttering, she tried not to wilt under his smoldering eyes. She only had seconds left with her fake boyfriend, and things had suddenly risen to a crescendo.

I stood on one train car and he stood on the other, both knowing that the cars had been disconnected and we'd be ripped apart at any second. I leaned forward, craving one simple kiss goodbye, and saw him leaning too. He said, "Daisy, are you listening? Hello?"

Daisy snapped out of her trance. "Yeah. What? I'm listening."

"Someday you have to tell me what's up, but before we stop—"

"Yeah?" She was leaning out of her doorway. Why was he taking so long to get to his point?

"When we get back to L.A., do you want—"

The door to the suite opened abruptly and Miss Dee hurried out with Pasha on her heels. "Mr. Gold himself is here to pick up Pasha. He's waiting in the front."

"Well, bye," he told Daisy, then quickly joining the hurry, he stepped into the hallway to lead the way out.

Daisy started to follow them. Maybe if she hung around with them on their way out, he'd have a chance to finish what he'd been about to say.

In the middle of the hallway, where the exit was, he took one lingering glance over his shoulder at Daisy, then picked up a suitcase from the luggage rack and carried it out the door.

Miss Dee said, "Pasha, do you have all of your things?"

"Yes, Miss Dee." She held up her tiny Moana suitcase and plush Moana doll.

Daisy followed them out of the train. On the platform, people were pouring out of every car, and in the activity, Cannon's attention was completely consumed.

"Goodbye, Daisy Mae," said Pasha, who had stopped, to the dismay of Miss Dee.

"Goodbye, Appassionata."

Again, Pasha came forward and gave her a hug. "I'm not s'pose to tell strangers this, but I ride the train back to Los Angeles next Friday. In case you wanna see us again."

"Maybe I will see you," said Daisy. "Thanks for teaching me Mancala."

"You're welcome. Bye." She waved and Miss Dee tilted her head in farewell as they walked off.

Cannon turned his head, gave her another wink and then she was forgotten.

What had he been about to say? And why was the timing so crappy?

Oh well, it was probably for the best. Never again would she be involved with a man who put her so low on his list of priorities and she had serious doubts about Cannon. With a sigh for what might have been, Daisy pulled out her phone to call Maia and find out where to meet her.

5

Cannon hauled the last two sheets of drywall into the small addition to the church and laid them on top of the pile. The church was relatively new, and some parts of the building were still only framed out. This addition would be a room built specifically to be a nursery, so parents could worship and study while their kids were taught and cared for here. After catching a red-eye back to L.A. Saturday night, he'd slept a few hours, gone to services, then slept some more. Monday morning he was refreshed and ready to get to work on this project.

Blayze, one of his SEAL Team 7 buddies, pulled the trigger on the drill and said, "You slap 'em up, and I'll drill 'em in."

"Thanks again for giving me a hand," said Cannon, lifting one sheet and carrying it to the far corner and lifting it flat against the studs in the ceiling.

"I didn't have much of a choice with that guilt trip you took me on."

Blayze sunk a couple of drywall screws and Cannon went for the next piece while Blayze completed that sheet. After years of training together and working on covert operations, they didn't need to talk to complete such a basic task.

"So," said Cannon, going for another sheet, "how are things with ... what's her name again?"

Blayze growled. "Don't bother learning it. We're done."

"Done? You barely started."

"Don't remind me," said Blayze, using the drill to take his frustration out.

They continued to work, complementing each other and finishing the ceiling in record time.

"So what's the issue," asked Cannon, lifting a sheet and carrying it to the corner of the wall. "Why don't your relationships last?"

"Oh, no," said Blayze, shaking his head. "I came here to do drywall, not be psychoanalyzed."

Cannon chuckled silently. The hostage-negotiation-slash-human-polygraph guy hated it when people tried to get inside his head. Still, even if Cannon couldn't help Blayze work out his issues, he knew it was good for his buddies to get together once in a while and just hang out, or even better, give service.

What Cannon didn't tell any of them, was that he needed time with them once in a while. When he was with his SEAL buddies, it was easy to be the happy one, the one who always thought life was great and the future was bright. What they didn't know was that when he didn't have the role to fill on the team, everything was different. All the darkness he'd seen and experienced grew inside him and sometimes made it hard to see the light.

It was the same feeling when he was around Daisy, but times a million. Like all was right in the world. He didn't know what it was about her personality, but he'd never felt like that before. In the few days since the train trip ended, he'd even considered going to Sutton Smith, the Warrior Project leader, and asking for help tracking her down since he had seemingly limitless resources.

The Warrior Project had been started by Sutton to honor his son

Doug's death. Sutton invited five former SEALs from Doug's platoon to help him right some wrongs. They didn't always operate strictly within applicable laws but they always did what they could for people in situations with no one else to turn to. Like Rasmus Gold, who couldn't just call up Bodyguards"R"Us to get the exact guy he needed.

A quick double-tap *zip-zip* with the drill brought Cannon back to the present. Blayze was waiting for the next sheet. They finished hanging all the drywall quickly and as Cannon started sweeping up, Blayze grabbed his keys and water bottle.

"Wanna grab lunch?" asked Cannon.

"Can't," said Blayze. "Meeting with Sutton today."

"New job? Must not be something urgent or you'd be running out the door." Since Blayze was the hostage negotiation expert, he was the most likely guy to be picked up in a helicopter and flown out somewhere.

"Yeah, nothing urgent, I'm sure, but I don't know what yet."

"All right," said Cannon. "Thanks again. I'll let you know when we start drywalling the basement."

Blayze laughed and waved it off, but he froze in the door. "Sorry I can't make it to lunch, brother, but let's watch the Clippers game tomorrow."

"Cool," said Cannon.

Still Blayze stood there, forming his thoughts. "I know it's hard for you to keep the lights shining all the time, Big Gun. When you don't have the job to do for your buddies, it can be hard to do for yourself. Stay in touch. Reach out." Blayze walked out without another word.

How in the world had he figured that out about Cannon? Yeah, reading people was his specialty, but still. Was Cannon that transparent?

The worst part of it was, his buddies weren't always around. Corbin had Delaney, and River was in Hawaii on assignment. The job with Pasha was such a blessing, and it was easy to slip back into that role when he was being her best friend and protector, but that was only two days a week.

Maybe God had something else in store. Maybe that something else would include a certain blonde with a smile like the sun. It couldn't be that hard to find Editor Daisy Close even in a big city, could it? He'd give her a week or so to return from her trip to Seattle and then he'd start tracking her down.

Cannon checked his watch. He was leading a youth Bible study tonight for the first time and wasn't sure if he was ready. Just thinking about it made his palms sweat on the broom handle. His volunteer position as lay pastor was proving to be challenging in ways he'd never expected. He still didn't know if he was trying to counteract the darkness from his life, or just trying to focus on the good in the world and help other people do the same. Most likely a combination of the two, but the fact that he was so uncomfortable doing it, meant he needed more of it in his life.

Like Daisy. For the millionth time in three days, he thought about how much he needed Daisy.

6
_____

Six days after arriving in Seattle, Daisy hopped out of Maia's car at the King Street Train Station. Her original plan had been to fly back to L.A., but ever since Pasha had mentioned the return trip today, Daisy had been reconsidering. When she realized the only way she'd see Cannon again was on the train, her decision was made and she booked another ticket on the Coast Starlight. Maybe her newfound sister and her almost boyfriend would be on board, and maybe they wouldn't be. Only one train departed for L.A. each day, so it was worth a shot just for the chance.

This time she'd booked a roomette, and was directed by the attendant on her car to one of the upstairs rooms. Once again she'd lucked out and was on the side of the train that would allow her a view of the ocean once they got to Southern California, but she was on a different car altogether from her last trip. If she remembered right, Pasha's suite was on the bottom deck of the car in front of hers. No, behind hers, since they were traveling south instead of north. Or did it all flip around entirely? She'd have to find out.

Either way, she didn't want to go knocking on their door and impose on them first thing. So she got settled into her room, set up her laptop and was already deep into an edit before the train pulled out of the station. She knew where they'd likely be at six o'clock, so in the meantime she'd get as much work done as the passing view of Seattle would allow.

The car was relatively quiet but people passing in the hallway kept distracting her as she looked up, hoping to see Cannon, so she pulled the curtain closed. The view of the city gave way to open grassland, forests, and towns as the train motored down the track. She could get used to this life.

When the dining car attendant came through taking dinner reservations, she felt a rush of excitement when he confirmed that there were still six-o'clock slots open. Daisy went back to work with a renewed rush of energy. The book was fascinating, which made it easy to get into, but with the prospect of seeing her former fake boyfriend again, she was energized.

The book was a thriller by Camille Jackson about two sisters, separated at birth and ignorant of the other's existence. When one commits murder, the other is charged for it based on DNA evidence. The writing was impressive, the motives made Daisy feel torn, and the characters themselves were complex and gripping. The big flaw with the book was that it was based on outdated science that said identical twins had identical DNA, which had been solidly refuted in recent years.

It wasn't Daisy's job to solve the problems, just point them out. Knowing Camille, she'd find a solution that was even more brilliant than her original premise.

When they started calling dinner reservations at 5:00, Daisy couldn't believe how late it had gotten. The sun was thinking about dipping behind the horizon and sunlight was blaring in through her window. Without even realizing it, Daisy had taken up a stance to block the sun from washing out her screen by putting the back of her laptop to it.

For the next hour she worked her way through the lives of Robin and Rebecca, but by the time the six o'clock call came, she was right in the middle of the climax. She closed her laptop and stood to stretch as much as her room would allow, and remembered she hadn't dressed for dinner yet. She only had the one sun dress with her, but she had enjoyed dressing up a little for the formal dinner, and even though she might not fit in with the random dinner companions she ended up with tonight, she still put the dress on. And touched up her makeup. And ran a brush through her hair. And popped a Tic-Tac in.

By the time she approached the dining car, it was 6:10. As soon as she walked in to the car, she saw Miss Dee sitting at the first table on the left, this time wearing a gray business suit with a skirt. It took half a second for her to place Daisy, but when she did, she smiled warmly. Pasha was next to her, and noticed her next.

"Daisy!" Pasha looked briefly for an escape route to come hug her, but settled on a big wave. She was wearing a gorgeous red dress with roses on the bodice and a bow on the high waist.

"Hey, sis," said Daisy, coming to stand next to the table.

She approached slowly on purpose, savoring the anticipation of seeing Cannon again. And there he was. His suit was black again, and he looked even more like an international spy than she remembered with his good looks, great style, and relaxed air.

Her plan had worked! She almost jumped into the air right there in the dining car.

For half a second he looked pleased to see her, then his smile shifted slightly to become ... suspicious. "Daisy," he said, with a tip of the head. He looked her over, but not in the creepy way a guy would check her out. Now that she knew who he was, she knew she was being scanned more thoroughly than a TSA security check. Good thing she had left her bazooka back in L.A.

"Hi, Cannon," said Daisy. "Miss Dee."

"Hello," said Miss Dee.

"I was hoping you'd come," said Pasha.

"Me too," said Daisy. "I want a Connect Four rematch with you."

"If you want to," said Pasha, "but I don't know if it'll be fun. I figured out how to win every time, even against Miss Dee, but only when I go first."

Cannon rose from his seat and Miss Dee said, "Would you please join us?"

"Oh, I didn't want to impose." Why had Miss Dee been the one to offer if Cannon was the one making room for her? She hadn't seen any unseen signal pass between the two of them.

"Pleeeeease," said Pasha, but on a look from Miss Dee, she amended it to, "We would be very pleased if you joined us for dinner."

"How can I say no to that invitation?" asked Daisy, sliding in to the window seat.

And just like that, she found herself side to side with her new boyfriend and across from her charming little sister. Again, Pasha interviewed her over dinner, but this time she was prepared. And this time, she was sitting next to Cannon, which was electrifying. It was harder to see him, but his mere presence had her buzzing inside.

She focused on the well-crafted questions she'd prepared to learn more about her train boyfriend. "What do you want to be when you grow up?" asked Daisy.

"Either President of the United States or a pediatric surgeon."

That was much more specific than Daisy had imagined. It almost knocked her off her game, but she responded, "I would vote for you. Or take my kids to you if they ever needed surgery." Before Pasha could go on to another question, she asked, "Do you know where you want to go to college?"

"Probably Harvard or Oxford," said Pasha confidently.

Daisy struck with her follow up question before Pasha had a

chance to get the interview back on track. "What about Miss Dee and Cannon? Where did they go to college?"

"Miss Dee went to …" she considered for just a moment, then said, "Norland College. It's in England and it's the best school for nannies in the world. That's why she's such an amazing nanny. And Cannon was a soldier before he became my best friend."

Ex-military. That made sense. Of course if he'd been in the Marines then it would be former Marine, since *Once a Marine always a Marine*. The things she picked up editing.

"What are your hobbies?" asked Pasha.

Daisy had lost the upper hand. "I love reading. Swimming in the ocean. But my favorite is probably singing."

Pasha responded, "I enjoy playing games, I enjoy hosting tea parties, and I enjoy coloring anatomy coloring books."

Wow, this girl was ready for life, no matter which profession she chose. "What about Miss Dee and Cannon?"

That one was tougher, and Pasha had to consider. "I believe Miss Dee likes to do gardening because you should see her flowers at Mother's house. And she is really, really good at cricket. She even taught me how to play. And golf, wow. If she wasn't my nanny, I know she'd be an LPGA. She plays the flute, too, and it is beautiful. Like a choir of birdies."

Oh was that all? Daisy didn't feel intimidated *at all*.

"Oh," said Pasha, "and she likes to paint. She gave a painting to … The Queen, and the Queen hung it up in her palace. She's teaching me to paint. Even though I can beat her in Connect Four now if I go first, I don't think I'll ever be as good at painting."

"Thank you, Miss Pasha," said Miss Dee. "That's very kind of you to say."

Daisy wondered if she had to prompt Pasha to tell her about Cannon, but Pasha was a strong enough conversationalist that she went back on topic.

"Now Cannon," she said, sounding like an exasperated adult.

"He doesn't really do anything other than look around all the time. Sometimes he plays games with me, but he's always so distracted he's not very good."

"That's not very nice," said Miss Dee.

"I'm sorry, Cannon," Pasha told him. "What I meant was, he has other strengths beside playing games. Oh! You should hear him sing. He's even better than the guy who sings the *Toy Story* song, 'You Got a Friend in Me'."

Cannon chuckled, a rare break in his demeanor. Was he blushing? Daisy was pretty sure he was.

Pasha rolled her eyes. "I'd ask him to sing now, but he never does except at bedtime."

"A soldier and a singer?" said Daisy. "That's every girl's dream guy right there."

Daisy studied him and noticed a slight squirm to his normally soldier-straight posture and there were red spots showing up on his cheeks. Miss Dee raised an eyebrow at him in a very British way, killing the connection between them. It was Miss Dee who Daisy needed to get out of the picture, not Pasha. Well, not get out of the picture like *that*. She just wanted more alone time.

Pasha didn't notice any of the exchange. She grinned lovingly up at Cannon, who said, "I'm lucky to have such a smart, polite, and pretty best friend."

Pasha looked at Daisy and said, "I don't know what Cannon does when I'm at Mother's or Father's house." In a fake whisper with her mouth covered with the back of her hand, she said, "I think he just sits there and looks around the room."

Again he laughed along with Daisy.

For the rest of the meal, she continued to pick up tidbits about her on-again boyfriend, but since Pasha only saw him on the train, she knew surprisingly little about him. Still it was an enjoyable dinner in the company of this little pseudo family that had taken her in.

After dinner, Pasha performed a short poem—"Ridiculous Rose" by Shel Silverstein—and did it in an entirely different character than she'd done "Jabberwocky".

As they stood from the table, Pasha invited Daisy to watch *Frozen* with them. It had been years since Daisy had seen it, and even in his reticent state, Cannon was fun to be around, so she put off the twins and their legal and familial issues to join them. Pasha showed up in *Frozen* pajamas, but Cannon and Miss Dee both wore their normal business attire. Daisy was thinking like Pasha and wore sweat pants and a sweat shirt.

As expected, Cannon sat in the back corner of the room and didn't speak to anybody. Even though Daisy never felt unsafe on the train, having him back there guarding the room make her feel all warm and protected. After the movie, they went their separate ways. And as before, there was a hug and a goodnight from Pasha but nothing but a momentary glance and a smile from Cannon.

Was it just her or was he colder toward her than the last train trip? Did he see her as a bother? A threat? Despite her intentions, maybe she really had imposed on their hospitality, even though she was paying her own way this time.

Oh well, at least the twins were waiting for her back in her room.

7

Cannon sat staring down the dimly lit hallway of the sleeper car. He couldn't believe Daisy was back on the train with them. It'd been like a Christmas morning surprise when she'd popped in at dinner, and he'd learned even more about her than last trip, but not being able to interact directly with her was taking all of the discipline he could muster, and that was saying a lot for a former SEAL. She was an entirely different distraction than anything he'd ever faced, and he was starting to wonder if someone was behind it. Not as a way to get to Pasha, merely to find out what it would take to get his defense of Pasha to drop.

Rasmus Gold was shrewd and smart enough to try something subtle like this as a test. Heck, Sutton might even throw something like the perfect woman at him.

From everything Cannon knew about Daisy, she was everything he wanted in a woman: intelligent, kind, playful, great with kids, and gorgeous. But more than anything, it was easy for him to see the good in the world when she was around. He still didn't know why or how, but she made him all giddy inside. He'd never even thought that word before, but it was the only way to describe how she made him feel. She was pure and childlike and innocent. Again, like no one he'd ever known.

Maybe it was because there was no darkness in her that he was able to only see the good in the world with her around.

Someone was coming down the stairs. At midnight, it was probably a passenger from the upper level up for a bathroom break. There was a bathroom in the upper level, but it got more usage than the downstairs restrooms, so quite a few people made the trip down where there were two restrooms to split the customers and fewer sleeper rooms down here to begin with. Therefore, cleaner restrooms.

The rhythm of the steps was familiar. A large person, but with quick, comfortable steps. It was a game he played, trying to guess as much as he could about the person before he saw them.

This one was easy—Terrell, the attendant. Cannon knew it before he came around the corner.

Sure enough, the big guy rounded the corner, holding a pot of coffee. "How you doing, my man?" he asked Cannon. No one else was up and about in the car.

Cannon kept one eye on the hallway as he talked in low tones with Terrell. "It's another beautiful night. How bout you?"

"I'm going to catch a few hours sleep. Thought I'd top you off."

"Thanks, man," said Cannon, removing the lid from his cup and holding it out. The dark coffee steamed as it filled Cannon's cup. The aroma worked wonders on Cannon's weary mind. During the day there was always coffee available upstairs, but Cannon was tied to his post down here and Terrell knew that. He also knew Cannon would be awake through the night, so he kept the coffee on longer than he did on typical trips and came down every few hours.

"No cream or sugar?" asked Terrell. He knew Cannon took his coffee black, but always offered anyway.

Cannon shook his head.

"Aight, anything else you all need?"

Not unless you can take my post for the night so I can go find Daisy and see if she's up for a late-night conversation. "Nah, we're good for tonight." He capped his coffee cup and cheers'd him. "Thanks, Terrell."

He grunted as he turned to go back upstairs.

Sitting back in his seat, Cannon sniffed the steam coming through the hole in his cup. Terrell wasn't as trusted and trained as James, the southbound kitchen attendant, or Gustav, the northbound guy, but Cannon had known him long enough that he didn't turn down a cup of coffee. If anyone ever did plot against Pasha and her parents enough to poison Cannon or even knock him out for the night, Miss Dee could hold her own against most threats. She was trained in firearms and in self-defense and always had a .357 Smith and Wesson within reach.

They didn't mess around at Norland College. Pretty much all of the British royalty employed nannies from Norland, and while the position with Pasha wasn't as prestigious as the royalty jobs, it paid better. Miss Dee made a lot more than Cannon, and he was in six-figures for his two-day-a-week gig. They both had all of their expenses covered while on duty, and Cannon got unlimited airfare between Seattle and L.A. in between train trips, plus housing in Seattle when he decided to stay there rather than fly back home.

Cannon sipped his coffee, then set it aside. Even though he trusted Terrell, he always took a sip then let it sit for at least 20 minutes to see if he had any adverse consequences. Tonight he probably didn't even need the coffee to stay awake since he was already energized by the hours he'd been able to spend with Daisy.

He pulled out his Bible and it fell open to a passage he'd read enough that he didn't really need the book. *I am not fit to untie the thong of his sandals.* That was John the Baptist. Then there was Peter.

Depart from me Lord, for I am a sinful man. If those two men weren't worthy, how could Cannon be worthy?

He popped his Bluetooth earpiece in and started his audiobook back up. *Dead Heat*, the seventh Harry Dresden novel.

Another set of footsteps sounded on the stairs. Cannon paused his book and listened. This one was slower and uneven with the slight jostling of the train. A woman, he guessed, mid-20s. Blonde hair, blue eyes, beautiful. Smile that could light up the room.

Oh boy, now Daisy was influencing his private little game.

But it *was* Daisy who came around the corner of the stairwell. Cannon shook his head to clear it and make sure he wasn't dreaming. He'd never fallen asleep on duty before, but this was just too good to be true.

Sure enough, it was Daisy, and she walked slowly toward him. Had Terrell really found her and asked her to come? No, Cannon thought back and he was sure he'd only thought that wish. Maybe God was working in his life and giving him a chance to do what he hadn't been able to at the end of their last trip.

Daisy was only a couple of feet away from his doorway when he said quietly, "Halt. Who goes there."

She didn't jump this time, just came slowly to a stop near his door. She was an angel, all pure smile, and good energy. "I was ready for you that time."

Grinning widely, he stood and stepped into the hallway. "You came back for more?"

"I've heard that soldiers get all inspired for their cause by pretty girls." She fidgeted a little, but pushed onward. "You got a tough job down here, so I thought I'd bring you something to help you through the night."

"What is it?" he asked, mind racing for what she could be talking about. Just the fact that she knew that he thought she was a pretty girl, as understated as that was, thrilled him.

"This," she said, turning her face to the light and smiling. Just smiling. She had come all the way down here just to bring him a smile.

Yes, that's what Cannon needed—a woman who could roll with life and see the joy and goodness in it. He felt all funny inside and had to admit, he was giddy. He almost got down on one knee and proposed marriage right then and there.

Was there something in the coffee?

No, he recognized that feeling from *Bambi*. He was twitterpated and it was a new feeling for him. In a voice low enough that it wouldn't wake anyone in the nearby rooms, he said, "I feel like I could sail the Seven Seas for a smile like that." Her dimple alone was worth any amount of treasure.

"Pirate theme tonight?"

"Huh? Oh, the halt and the sailing thing?" He really needed to practice talking to girls. Thinking quick he said, "I thought maybe you were editing a book about pirates and I'd help you stay in the mood."

"That's nice of you," she said. "But I'm editing this really good book, and it's just two tics off from being bestseller quality."

She seemed worried about something. "And?"

"I don't know," said Daisy. Her tone was conversational, in no hurry. "I'm not that far into the book, and I can't quite put my finger on what's up with it. It helps to step away and let it all settle in my brain to make sure I give the author the best feedback possible. I love how the bumps and turns of the train are like a mild shaker for my brain, helping the ideas to settle in so I can analyze them more clearly."

"Want to sit down?" asked Cannon.

"Sure," said Daisy, glancing inside his roomette.

It wouldn't work to have a woman in his room with him. "Here," he said, pulling back the partially drawn curtain on the roomette across the hall. "This one's empty."

"Wait, I stayed in the room you're in last time. Do you guys always travel with an empty room?"

"Are you prying? Should I be suspicious of you?" He was teasing but also watching her reaction.

"Me? No. I couldn't hurt anyone even to save a life."

She didn't show any of the signs of lying that Blayze had taught him, and Cannon's gut said she was definitely safe. Even if she did have evil intent, Cannon was confident he could protect himself and Pasha from anything Daisy and any possible conspirators had planned.

"We keep a room as a buffer for Pasha's suite." He didn't mention that he went back and forth between the two rooms to keep it fresh and confuse would-be threats.

"Thank you," said Daisy, accepting his offer to sit in the empty room. He carefully reached past her and turned on the night light in her room. It wouldn't do to have her in the dark and him in the light. He wouldn't be able to see her natural smile that she'd come all the way down here to give him.

"Tell me about the book." Cannon leaned against her door, facing the hallway.

She started with the characters, an old man and distant niece, gave the setting, the plot, going on and on. Cannon never wanted her to stop.

When she got to the end of her description, saying something about the cousins who hated the girl, Cannon asked, "Why?"

Again she started into more of the story, and talked for a couple minutes, then stopped suddenly. "That's it. It's their motivation. How did I not see that? Cannon, you are a genius! I could kiss you right now."

That sounded so tempting to Cannon, but he couldn't do it under the circumstances. But that didn't mean he couldn't look at her upward-turned lips and imagine what it would be like to kiss them. If her smile could inspire him to cross oceans, what would that kiss do for him?

"The smile was probably enough inspiration, but I'll take a rain check on the kiss." He was rewarded with another brilliant smile. He flushed and felt like his collar was too tight. Running his hand along the side of his hair he realized he still had the Bluetooth speaker in so he popped it out and tossed it back into his roomette.

"Were you listening to something?" she asked.

"Yeah. You know Jim Butcher?"

"Of course," said Daisy. "Harry Dresden Files?"

"Yeah, book seven." He didn't like looming over her in the hallway so he sat Indian-style on the floor of the hallway with his back facing the door of Pasha's suite. As quietly as they were talking, he was certain it wouldn't disturb Pasha or Miss Dee since they slept with a white-noise maker. "What else do you like to read?"

"I'm pretty wide read, but I do love anything with romance. Some of my favorites are Checketts, Hart, Youngblood, Krey."

"I have to admit," said Cannon, "I don't have a whole lot of experience with that." *The genre* or *the real thing*.

"What is it about Harry Dresden?" she asked. "I don't see you just blowing through it like pulp fiction."

"You're right," he said, amazed that she'd picked up on that. "He's one of my fictional heroes."

"Why?"

"He's just a normal guy, other than the fact that he's a wizard living in Chicago. He's so resourceful, and even though his weapons are a lot different than mine, since I don't know magic, he's always using something unexpected to overcome insurmountable odds. Plus, Harry's never corrupted by money or power, but always protects weaker people and women, no matter the cost."

Daisy had come forward on her seat, studying him. "That's the important part, isn't it? That last part."

How did she keep seeing so deeply into him? She was right,

though. He couldn't deny it. "Yeah, that's why he's one of my heroes." He looked up at the ceiling of the train, trying to decide how much to tell her. If he didn't tell her, she'd probably just figure it out. "I was reading about a couple other heroes earlier: John the Baptist and Peter. There's a balance to my life I think I've been trying to figure out for a long time. It's the balance of being worthy to be a man of God, but also strong enough to protect the weak at any cost, because I couldn't be the man I am today without going through what I've gone through in my life. It feels kind of like a paradox."

She waited for a second to make sure he was finished. Cannon could not believe he was opening up to her like this again. He didn't talk about this to anyone.

Daisy said, "It's what you told me last time we talked here. A battle between darkness and light."

"Yeah."

"I've thought about that," she said. "How can you fight the darkness, but remain in the light?"

"Yes!" he exclaimed quietly, coming up onto his knees. She actually understood. It was like a miracle and he wanted to complete the connection by taking her hands, pulling her in, and getting that kiss she'd promised. But this wasn't the time or place.

He did have to see her again, and he wasn't going to let her slip away like last time. This was an area he wasn't familiar with, and instead of proceeding with caution to avoid any pitfall, he just plunged ahead.

"Will you go out to dinner with me?"

Her mouth fell open, but she didn't speak. Her mouth twisted as she considered him.

"A date?"

"Yeah, a date?" Why was she hesitating? Had he picked up the wrong signals? He was suddenly very alert to their environment, since suddenly the world was askew.

"I ... want to, but I'm a little nervous."

"Why? I can line up a double date if being on a date with a guy you barely know makes you nervous. Or you can bring a couple friends. Or we could each bring a friend and make them go blind, or meet in a public place. Zane would be perfect. He looks like Thor, so if you've got a friend who's into superhero types—" He took a breath. "I'll stop rambling now." Hopefully Daisy wasn't into superheroes because Cannon couldn't take it if she started dating Blayze.

Daisy chuckled and said, "I'm not scared of anything like that." She paused again, studying his face with those incredible blue eyes. Even with her face backlit, he could see them glimmering.

"What's going through your mind?" he asked.

She let out a breath, "Oh, just trying to decide if I want to admit my insecurities to you."

"After all I've dumped in your lap about my darkness? Besides, I've already plunged into treacherous waters by asking you out," he admitted. "I'm really inexperienced at it."

The way her eyebrows went up made it clear she was surprised. "Okay, then I'll be honest with you." With the slightest defiant tilt to her chin, she said, "I don't want you to be distracted."

Cannon was no expert on psychology and reading body language—but he'd had enough training crammed into him to know instinctively that what she said was important to her. He'd even go so far as to say all-important.

"You don't want me to be distracted?"

"That's right," she said. "If we go out, I want to be your date. I want to know I will be more important than everything else around you."

Oh, now he got it. She didn't like how he was so focused on security on the train, that they couldn't get close.

As if on cue, and with horrible timing, another set of footsteps started from the stairwell.

Cannon rose to his feet, and before the person made it to the bottom of the steps, he set his eyes firmly on hers and said, "I promise I will be all yours."

And just like that he had to look away from her again, right after promising she'd have his attention. From the corner of his eye he saw her scowl and retreat into the room.

That move, that promise, could have been smoother. His attention was definitely divided with her on the train, but his loyalties were clear. Pasha was the only thing that mattered. If he could get Daisy on a date, he could prove how much he cared about her and only her.

The guy finished in the bathroom and went back upstairs, but Daisy was already standing to go. She held out a business card and he saw a phone number on it.

"I smell coffee," she said. "You need a refill?"

"Got one right before you came," he said. "But I don't need it."

"No?"

Cannon shook his head. "I got your smile, remember?"

That earned him another smile, sending electricity coursing through his body.

"Goodnight," she said, turning to leave.

"Goodnight," he said, savoring the intimacy this time.

At the stairwell, she paused and turned her head back over her shoulder. Cannon winked, and she disappeared.

A date. They were going on a real date. And he could prove to her that he could put her first.

Cannon couldn't remember ever being this excited for a mission.

8

R ed flag! Red flag! Red flag! Not two seconds after promising to give her all his attention on their future date, she was all but ignored.

Was there some threat she couldn't see? Were their lives in danger? Was she overreacting because her made-up boyfriend was doing his job?

Yes to that last one. The other questions she couldn't answer. But she'd give him a chance on a date when he wouldn't have an excuse. And if she didn't get his attention at that point, she could walk away. Not only *could* she walk away, she *would* walk away. She wouldn't hang around for three years with hopes of the future.

She heard steps in the hallway and peeked around the corner to see a middle-aged man duck into the restroom. Cannon must have sensed him coming. Some sort of Spidey-sense or something. With his attention divided—no that was the wrong word—with his attention *elsewhere*, she didn't want to talk to him.

True, he'd done the exact same thing before when someone

appeared—basically prepared for a fight. It was just the timing that made her feel like she had a pit sitting in her stomach.

Daisy didn't know what she'd say once they were alone again. With the date planned it was almost as if she didn't want to get all the talking done. There were still a million things she wanted to know about him, and she really doubted she could get sick of learning more about him, but now that the date was set, any more conversation felt premature.

Reluctantly, she stood, but waited until the gentleman had come out of the restroom and returned to the upper level so she knew he was paying attention to her. She gave him her card so he could get in touch with her and offered to get him some coffee.

He told her he didn't need it because, "I got your smile, remember?"

She felt relief that her silly, confident plan had worked on him, but she also felt a rush of pleasure that he liked her smile.

All she could say was, "Goodnight."

"Goodnight," he told her in a smoldering voice, and she felt it all the way down to her toes.

As she was about to head up the stairs, she glanced back and caught a wink.

Daisy had to pinch herself to keep from fading into fantasy land. She'd already gone mentally AWOL on him once this conversation.

As she made it upstairs and back to her car, she thought about their conversations, laughing when she thought about him rambling and all his ideas to make the date safe for her. He was so cute and confident and strong and somehow nervous about asking her out.

Inside her room, Daisy did an ungraceful spin, giggling and putting a hand to her chest. She wanted to sing, but it was much too late. His handsome face was front and center in her mind and she loved it. Never in a million years did she think she'd be twirling and giggling on a train, but Cannon was worth it with his James Bond looks, and mysterious, brooding dark past, and the intensity he body-guarded with.

She let out a wistful sigh ... admitting to herself that she really did like him and if things didn't go well on the date, it could be bad. But in the meantime she'd keep hoping this fake boyfriend could turn into something real.

9

Daisy waited in the lobby of Outback Steakhouse two days after the train arrived in L.A. She was fifteen minutes early and couldn't wait to discover what she would find in her maybe boyfriend without all the distractions.

They hadn't driven together because Daisy had a thing about getting in a guy's car on a first date, even though it wasn't technically their first time being together. If she still felt okay with him after their date, she'd get a ride home with him. Besides she was only a few blocks from home and her roommate had been heading out anyway.

With ten minutes left before the time they'd planned to meet, Cannon walked in the door.

All of a sudden Daisy's heart was beating a thousand times a minute and she could feel her eyes go all dreamy.

When the door opened, a marble statue in a sweater walked in. Only a Renaissance sculptor could craft facial features so defined and manly...

Daisy pinched her thigh as she stood up. She expected she'd be using that trick around Cannon a lot to stay in the here and now.

Her hopefully boyfriend was wearing a gray sweater over some loose fit jeans. He was clean shaven, as usual, and his hair was styled slightly messy, taunting her to run her fingers through it. And those emerald eyes. She had to pinch herself again. Daisy was glad she'd worn a dress—a teal and brown herringbone maxi—because she felt like she and Cannon just went well together.

"You look amazing," said Cannon, opening his arms and bringing her in for a hug. She gladly reciprocated.

When my arms touched his back, it was like hugging a demi-god. Strength poured from him in waves and I had to hold on to keep from being washed away. But in his power there was gentleness and joy, and he held me like a precious gem.

When he released her, Daisy stepped back and looked up into his eyes again. It was every bit as magical as her fantasy had been. With Cannon, she didn't need to go away to another world, because what could be better than the perfect mix of strength and softness she got with him?

From the moment he walked in, his eyes hadn't gone anywhere but to her. Her boyfriend was back. And where had that sense of strength come from? It wasn't his muscles, wait, it was his muscles, but it was more. She could sense inner strength as if he had a lion's heart beating in his chest.

"Mind switch?" he asked with that amused smile.

Daisy blushed, and rolled her eyes in embarrassment, but deep down she loved that he could recognize it, even if he didn't know exactly what was going on.

Cannon broke the connection momentarily to check in with the hostess, who had their table ready and showed them back. A booth would have been more intimate for the date, but at least the table gave them more chances for distractions. TVs blared in every direction, some men at the nearby bar were loudly into a game, most of the other tables were full, and servers walked by constantly.

"I hope Outback is okay?" he said, after pulling her chair out for her. "I saw you eat salmon and steak on the train, plus there's a bar here and I didn't know if you were a drinker or not."

"Sometimes," she said, reveling a little in his awkwardness. "Not so much on first dates." With all the distractions, still, Cannon seemed to notice only her and it was clear he was out of his element in the dating world. He made the most irresistible fish out of water she'd ever seen, and yet he still wore that smile like everything was right in the world.

"Same here," he said. "I'll admit I've got some nerves running sharp, but it wouldn't be worth dulling them at the risk of drowning any of my common sense."

Daisy took his hand and felt the tension case out. Her own body came alive at his touch.

He let out a breath. "Thanks."

"What would you tell Pasha if she was nervous about a new situation?"

"That girl?" He chuffed. "She eats new situations for breakfast."

"Okay what if she was scared? All little girls get scared sometimes."

"Scared?" He said the word like it was new to him. "I'm not scared. But if Pasha was, I'd sing her a song."

Daisy was dying to hear him sing. "Why?" she asked.

"To take her mind off whatever was bugging her. To let her know someone had her back."

That was so precious, but before she could respond, the server walked up. She was a cute blonde who could have passed for Daisy's younger, cuter, perkier sister. She was wearing a button-down shirt, that was not only too tight for her, but also buttoned down at least one button more than Daisy would be comfortable with. Another great test of his attention to Daisy. She had to squeeze Cannon's hand to get him to even notice someone had come up to their table. Wow. Her new boyfriend was seriously into her.

They both ordered water, but asked the server to give them a few minutes since neither of them had picked up a menu. Again, his eyes never left Daisy's as the waitress swayed away from them.

They took a minute to figure out what they wanted, then he said, "Tell me about yourself."

"Me? You already know my life story thanks to your little interviewer. The only thing I know about you is that your only hobby is to sit in a room and look around."

He laughed, that magical and genuine movement. Daisy started to float away to her fantasy land but pinched herself in time.

"She's something else, isn't she? What do you want to know about Cannon Culver?"

"Your name is an oxymoron," she told him.

"Oxymoron," he said slowly, and she could see the files opening and closing in his mind as he searched for the literary definition.

"It's a phrase that contradicts itself," she said. "Like little giant, or the living dead. Culver means dove, which is the sign of peace. So basically your name is Big Gun Peace."

His eyebrows went up. "The guys in my platoon call me Big Gun, and I do love the idea of a forceful and fierce path to peace. I think you're the first person to ever figure that out about my name, though. I was like 25 when I realized it."

"I do work with words for a living so I pick up on that."

"You should meet my brother Warsong and my sister Pike. My parents did it on purpose."

"For reals?"

"For reals," he said.

The guys at the bar came out of their seats and high fived each other. Cannon didn't so much as glance at them. In a booth on the other side of the room, a group of servers started loudly singing a happy birthday song, but Cannon might as well have been deaf. The server came back to the table and Cannon seemed to have to force his eyes away from Daisy's.

They put in their orders and he turned all the way back to Daisy.

She'd never felt so special in anyone's eyes, and imagined herself standing on a pedestal.

"I know you're from L.A.," said Cannon. "Do you have brothers and sisters?"

Daisy started to roll her eyes, but caught herself. "One sister and two parents. I don't get along all that great with any of them."

"I can't imagine you not getting along with anyone," he said. "You're like ... an angel."

That wasn't true, but dang it felt good to have a guy feel that way about her.

"I won't bore you with details, but Talia was the Olympic-hopeful gymnast. She never made it, but she was an alternate more than once. It just seemed like the Close Family Culture was Talia. Everything revolved around her." That didn't paint Daisy in a very good light. "Maybe I'm being petty, but I was always a side note since my singing career never had the same potential."

"Tell me more about your singing. What would it take to get you to belt something out?"

She laughed. "No way. Some other time. It's just as a hobby, really." She smirked and said, "Not as good as you, I'm sure, if Pasha's right."

Cannon laughed. Oh how she loved it when he laughed. It was the layers to him, she thought. Easy-going, smiley guy on the outside, but underneath that there was a tough layer that he didn't show, and wasn't easy to get to. The tough layer kept the darkness from taking over, but it required a lot of control. When a laugh came out, it was uncontrolled and unforced, but oh so true.

"Now that I know you are a singer, I can't even conceive of singing for you." He took a drink of water. "Ask Pasha in a couple years and I bet she'll have a different opinion of my singing voice."

"Tell me about the military," she said. Maybe that would get back to the inner layers of Cannon Culver.

He shrugged and his eyes dropped to the table in front of him. A lifetime of emotion glassed them over in the few seconds that passed before he looked back up at her. She'd never seen him so serious; she'd actually caught him without the grin on his face. "Some guys who were only in for four or five years write entire books about it. I was in for ten. Even in a 36-hour train trip, I could only scratch the surface."

"That bad?"

The old Cannon came back instantly. Was this a mask? Or was this who he was now, but still had to keep some things way down deep?

"No, not at all. I mean, there was plenty of bad, but that is so inadequate of a description." He considered for a moment, then said, "Have you ever run a marathon or a 10k or anything?"

"Two marathons!" said Daisy.

"Was it bad?"

"No," she said, automatically thinking of the sense of accomplishment. Then Mile 15 came to mind, when she'd dropped the water cup at the aid station and decided not to go back for more. And as she thought of the running itself, as well as the months of training, her mind changed again. "There were more hard times than good times, but if I compare the good versus the bad, the good moments are so much more powerful. They're worth so much more that they completely outweigh the bad."

Cannon looked at her with ... adoration. "If I ever write my book, I'm putting that in there. No, actually if I just say that, I won't have to write a book."

Daisy chuckled nervously under the praise. "A marathon doesn't compare to a decade in the military."

"A marathon is the ultimate large-scale display of the indomitable human spirit. The Oakland Marathon ran under an overpass by my house when I was in high school. I wasn't the most social kid, but I'd go out and watch people for hours and feel like I was connecting with them more than I did with the kids on my own school bus, who I didn't know how to talk to."

"The indomitable human spirit?" repeated Daisy. "I love that." She wanted to know more about him and felt like she might actually be penetrating the inner crust again. "Do you still have a hard time talking to people?" There had been a couple of times where this strong, confident guy had fumbled when talking to her.

He got that amused, knowing smile, and she could tell he was going to say something ironic or teasing. "Only beautiful women."

Oh, Cannon, you charmer.

"Becoming a Navy Chaplain cured me of my reluctant tongue."

"Chaplain," exclaimed Daisy. "So maybe Peaceful Warrior isn't as ironic as I thought."

"Peaceful Warrior," he said, nodding. "I really like that."

"So you never fought? Didn't use guns or anything?"

Cannon chuckled, but there was no amusement in it, just warning for anyone who messed with him. "I admit I'm a peace-maker, but if anyone ever pushes me or my country to the plow-shares-into-swords mode, it's on. I'll avoid a fight, but once it starts, I intend to win."

"Oh." Daisy hadn't seen even a hint of that side of him as he'd interacted with Pasha on the train. After a little bit of internet research she'd discovered that Pasha was the only daughter of billionaire entrepreneur Rasmus Gold. Which meant that not only was Cannon the best in the business of private security, but also had a soft enough side to be a five-year-old's best friend. Could anyone ever be such a perfect mix of gentleness and strength?

The server arrived with the food—a steak for Cannon and grilled shrimp for Daisy. The garlic and pepper aromas made Daisy start to drool. She picked a skewer and lifted it toward her mouth, but froze when she noticed a strange look on Cannon's face. He was slowly pulling out his silverware, but he looked reluctant for some reason.

"Everything okay?" she asked.

"Oh, the food, yeah. But I have to admit something." He looked at her like he didn't know how to say what he needed to tell her. "I snooped in your bags. On the train."

"You … what?" Was this some kind of joke?

"When you went to the restroom on that first train trip, I went into your room and looked in your purse and carry on."

Daisy felt her mouth hanging open. She set the shrimp down and said, "What in the world makes you think you had the right?"

"I had to make sure you weren't going to hurt her?"

Pasha. Even though the little girl wasn't even at the restaurant, she was still coming between them. Well, technically, the deed had been done over a week ago. "Do I look like the type of person who would hurt a little girl?"

"No," said Cannon. "Which is why I had to be sure."

They stared at each other. Cannon hadn't said he was sorry and he didn't even look remorseful even though he'd voluntarily confessed.

"I've thought about what I did a lot since that day, and I'm still twisted around in my mind. I even talked to Sutton, my … boss, about it. He was behind me 100 percent. But I'm still torn. I can't tell you that I'm sorry, because I would do that same thing with any stranger. The only way to avoid having done that was to not invite you to stay in that room, and it would have been inhumane to leave you in your condition in coach."

It made sense, logically, but emotionally Daisy felt betrayed. He hadn't apologized.

"In my business, when someone doesn't do their job, people get killed. If anyone ever messes with Pasha, like a full-on attack, the chances are I'm sending them straight to hell. I'd die for her, Daisy. That's how much I care about her and about the sacred trust, as I see it, that I owe her."

So that did explain a little why he'd casually go through her bags, but she wasn't sure she got the sacred trust about his job. "You'd die over money? Or is your job a sacred trust or something?"

"Over my word," said Cannon. "I promised to keep her safe, no matter what. I don't take that lightly."

Daisy didn't know exactly how that made her feel. What if someday Pasha came between Cannon and her and he had to choose one or the other? She already knew what his choice would be. What else in his life would turn out to be more important than her? His job? His Dodgers obsession? His weekly golf game even if they hadn't been out on an actual date for over a month?

He's not Sterling, Daisy reminded herself. *Give him a chance.*

She slid one shrimp off the skewer and chewed it to give herself time to think. It wasn't as good as it would have been before he'd outed himself. Things weren't over between them, but a lot of the good he'd done by being all hers on this date so far had been undone.

"What is it?" she asked, staring into his eyes. "What is there inside of you that gives you such a strong sense of protection?"

One of the guys at the bar was blabbing something about, "... when I was a Navy SEAL, we shot first, asked questions later and ..." They were all getting drunker and louder, but the SEAL comment made Cannon wince, but just barely. So he *was* aware of what was going on in the restaurant, just not letting himself get distracted. That was even more touching to Daisy than thinking he was oblivious.

"I ..." he blew out a breath. "That's a deep question. Another idea for an entire book."

"Give me the teaser. The back cover blurb." She slid another shrimp off the skewer with her teeth.

Cannon slowly cut his steak as he thought, then took more time chewing a bite before answering. "When you tell someone you'll do something, you do it. If you are strong enough to protect yourself *and* someone weaker, you do it. Cannon Culver has a big heart ... but it's the heart of a warrior." He grinned at his own melodrama and said, "I'm sorry, but you asked for it."

Daisy was almost in tears over the emotional impact of what he'd said, and a little shaky. The puzzle pieces of Cannon were coming together and he was deeper than she ever imagined. She dabbed her eyes and took a few hidden breaths, then leaned forward, fixed her gaze on him, and drank him in. "I ... want to read that book."

Cannon leaned forward, standing somewhat, hands reaching up and cradling her face. Finally the stone veneer of him was crumbling completely and she was face-to-face with a flesh and blood man. Their lips drew closer, closer, closer, locked in a tortuously sweet eternity of ever nearer, but never touching. Then their lips met and his kiss was as soft and strong as she'd come to realize Cannon himself was.

The kiss only lasted a moment, a delicious moment, and as he backed away, she savored the tingling of her lips and the fading smell of his cologne.

"You with me?" Cannon was back in his seat, watching her with one eyebrow raised.

Daisy licked her lips and gulped. She hadn't even gone away that time to her fantasy land, but was still swooning in the aftermath of the kiss. "Yeah. You, uh, caught me by surprise there." The room had never swayed quite so pleasantly

Between wiping her eyes when he'd gotten all sweet and sexy, and now the kiss and feeling all flustered, Daisy needed a minute. "I'm gonna run to the restroom real quick." She popped another shrimp as she stood and started walking off, but then she thought of something so she turned back. "Can I trust you with this?" she asked, reaching for her small purse.

Cannon exhaled and said, "I deserve that one. Yes, I will protect it, but I won't snoop."

With a wink she turned away. It only took a few seconds to check the mirror and see that Daisy didn't look as flustered as she felt, so she went back out.

Cannon had gotten up and was standing near the loud guys at the bar. His back was to Daisy so he didn't see her approach. He was talking to the biggest, most intimidating of the group, a bald guy in a tank top with tattoos on his arms and neck.

"... Stolen Valor Act makes it illegal to benefit from claiming to be a SEAL. Now, my hearing's not what it used to be, so I probably heard you wrong, but if these guys are keeping your glass full because they think you're some sort of hero, and it's not true, that's a crime, my friend."

The bald guy had his back straight, staring down Cannon but Cannon stood there like he was having a conversation with a buddy. They were the same height with the guy sitting on that bar stool. Cannon pulled out his phone.

"What's your name, man? I've got the website right here, I can prove to your buddies you were over there."

Daisy couldn't see Cannon's face, but she could see the muscles around his eyes tighten.

The bald guy didn't say anything.

Cannon's cheek rose in a smile. "Unless I heard you wrong. Go ahead and correct me if I misheard you."

Why wasn't this huge guy coming out of his seat and giving it back to Cannon? I mean Cannon was intense, but the guy at the bar was bigger and Daisy had always thought of guys with neck tattoos as having nothing to lose.

"Yeah, you heard wrong," said the bald guy, looking like a puppy backing down from a big dog. With his eyes down still he looked side to side at his buddies. As he turned back to the bar, he said, "Get your ears checked or something."

"Sorry to bother you, buddy," said Cannon. He turned and escorted Daisy the short distance to their table. He had known she was there the whole time.

The old Cannon was back, life-is-good smile and all. But that wasn't the vibe he'd been putting out at the bar.

"How's your shrimp?" He scooped a bite of baked potato into his mouth.

"So good." It really was better now that she had kind of moved past the whole snooping thing. She wasn't ready to forget about it, but she'd keep seeing how this went as she kept an eye on him and his priorities.

The interaction at the bar still had her a little confused and she wondered how well she really knew him. But it wasn't like he'd freaked out and started a fight. Apparently he just wanted the loud drunk guy to admit he wasn't a Navy SEAL. They'd already been in deep conversations enough so Daisy passed on bringing it up again.

The dinner conversation was light and fun. She liked everything she learned about him and really wanted to know him even better. The guys at the bar kept talking in low tones and glaring at Cannon, but he didn't even seem to notice. When they got up and left, Daisy breathed a little sigh of relief, but Cannon still acted oblivious.

When they were done with dinner they ordered a Chocolate Thunder from Down Under to share. Sharing a desert was always a sign to Daisy that a first date had gone great. Of course, the kiss was a dead giveaway of that.

The kiss. So much better than any fantasy she could dream up.

While they waited for dessert, Daisy asked, "So what else did you do in the military, Peaceful Warrior?"

"After I was a chaplain, I was a weapons expert," he said with a light in his eyes. "Oh, we had the best toys."

"You miss that aspect of it?"

"I do," he said. "I still like gadgets, but the ones I play with now just aren't as effective. Or expensive."

"Like what?"

Out of nowhere he was holding a black grip thingy that fit all four of his knuckles.

"Brass knuckles?" asked Daisy.

"Better," said Cannon. His hand flexed ever so slightly and the device made a small electrical arc along the flat end. "Stun device."

"Wow, where did you ..."

It disappeared as quickly as it had appeared, tucked into a pocket maybe. "I'm kind of a big nerd about stuff like that."

"What else do you have?"

"I'm not just going to flash all my goods out there on the first date," he said with mock shock, but he did nod her over so they were both leaning over the side of the table looking at his shoes. They were nice dress shoes, but she didn't see anything special.

Then he lifted his heel and some small, hard ridges appeared through the laces all along the tongue.

"What the?"

Cannon said, "Those give a little more punch to my kicks, no pun intended."

"I bet that comes in handy a lot," she said as a joke.

She expected a courtesy chuckle out of him since he was so spare with his laughs, but he just said, "A few times, actually. I do some ... odd jobs sometimes."

Daisy chuckled. "I'm not sure odd is the right word, but why do you carry those around and go through the trouble on a normal day?

His smile turned amused. "The way I see it, the only reason so many of us get to enjoy this wonderful world is because of people who are willing to step into the line of fire to defend the rest of us. Soldiers and cops mostly. I'm neither of those, but if anything ever goes down near me, I'll step up."

"You are so stinking humble," she said. "Oh, and what you just said ... that's totally going in the book I'm going to write about you."

Now he did laugh. "When you write your book, I'll point you to real heroes." His eyes went vacant for a minute, then he was the one blinking and trying to pretend like he was tougher than he actually was.

"You were thinking of someone right there."

"Doug Smith," said Cannon solemnly. "I wouldn't be sitting here today if he hadn't ..." He let out a long breath. "It was an ambush. Doug acted quickly and selflessly, knowing he'd never survive. But his actions, his sacrifice, saved over a dozen SEAL lives that day."

Daisy had to wipe her own eyes again. She didn't even know Doug Smith, but she felt eternally grateful to him.

"Sorry," said Cannon. "Too deep."

"No, I—"

The server came back with dessert, and the conversation stalled as they filled their mouths with chocolate thunder.

The restaurant was hopping, and Daisy hated to take up a table when the server had more tipping customers waiting to be seated.

"We should head out," she told him.

Cannon slipped some cash into the bill folder and held out his hand. "Your chariot awaits."

She loved the feel of his strong hand, so gentle with her, but pulsing with potential energy.

It was a beautiful night out.

"Walk along the beach?" he offered.

"Yes, that sounds perfect." She could walk hand-in-hand with him all night long.

Within a few minutes, they were on the sand, finally escaping the glaring lights of the city.

Their pace was slow and comfortable.

"How long have you lived in Southern California?" she asked.

Before he could answer, someone yelled, "Hey!"

Half a dozen men came toward them, outlined by the lights behind them and even though Daisy couldn't see them, she knew it was the huge drunk guy from the bar and his buddies.

Cannon stepped in front of her. "Keep walking," he told the guys. "Nothing to see here." His voice was soothing and convincing.

"There is something to see here," said the leader. "Me kicking your butt."

The guys were only about ten feet away. A couple of them were carrying bottles of beer.

Cannon said, "I don't want any trouble. You tell me which way you're going and we'll go the other direction."

Daisy considered pulling out her cell phone and calling the police but Cannon was so calm and confident, she just felt like he had this under control. He'd talk their way out of this, the peace-maker that he was.

The big guy came right up into Cannon's face. "You think you're all tough? You probably aren't even a SEAL. Let's see your proof." The rest of the group formed a half-circle around them.

"I never said I was a SEAL," said Cannon. "Now if you'll excuse us," he started to lead Daisy out of trap the men had formed, but the big guy shoved him. Cannon wasn't even knocked off balance.

"You're not excused," the big guy said, bringing a round of laughter from his buddies.

"I don't want a fight," said Cannon, facing them but trying to back away with Daisy in a safe position behind him.

"Of course you don't," said the big guy. "Cause you're gonna lose." He pointed with both hands, and his friends spread the circle out wider, cutting off almost all directions of escape.

Cannon was rigid and poised, she could feel him tensing like a snake preparing to strike. He was calm but threatening as he said, "Listen, friend. This is the last time I'm going to say this. Walk away. Don't say another word. Just turn around unless you want to get hurt." There was no more negotiator, just a soldier giving orders. Moving backwards and to the side, he stayed between Daisy and the men as he guided her away.

The big guy said, "Fine you go. We'll just keep your woman here with us and—"

From five feet away, Cannon shined a flood light right in the man's face, and when the guy lifted an arm to block his eyes, Cannon was there, shoving the flashlight into the guy's neck. It crackled with electricity. The guy shook and fell to the ground. Cannon dropped the flashlight and it ended pointing up at him like a spotlight. The knuckle device was on one hand, but he had a short rod in the other. With a flick, he extended it to about three feet, and jabbed another guy in the gut. Another crack of electricity and that guy went down, twitching as well.

With another flick, he closed the baton and hurled it at a guy on the other side of the semi-circle who had started closing in, smacking him on the head and sending him reeling backward. The closest guy to him tried to throw a punch, but Cannon spun behind him. Before Daisy knew what was happening, the guy was flying through the air. He came down hard, landing head first in the sand.

Only three guys were left standing. Cannon darted forward and decked one right in the nose, sending him flying back.

Two more, one on either side of him. The guy in front came forward ready to hit Cannon with a beer bottle. Did he see the guy behind him?

Before Daisy could call a warning, Cannon back-kicked the guy so hard in the chest he went reeling back into the surf. Then Cannon grabbed the wrist holding the bottle and snapped it with a sharp blow from his elbow. The crack echoed across the beach. Cannon dipped down and came up with an uppercut that lifted the guy off the ground.

"Snicker-snack," he said, then the guy landed with a thump.

By now, two guys were trying to get up. As graceful as a dancer, Cannon stepped twice and bent to pick up that baton, flicking it open and popping each guy with a jolt of electricity.

Daisy found herself wrapped in one of Cannon's arms, staring up into his chiseled face. He hadn't even broken a sweat and wasn't breathing hard, but Daisy was completely out of breath.

"Daisy? Are you okay?"

Had that fight really just happened? Daisy was still a little terrified, but also excited that her bodyguard boyfriend had just singlehandedly taken on a gang all by himself.

Still confused, she asked, "Did you ... say, 'snicker-snack'?"

Cannon grinned guiltily and nodded. "Couldn't resist."

So that part of the fight really had happened. Daisy glanced around and saw half a dozen men lying in the sand in various uncomfortable positions. That was no fantasy; it had really happened.

"Are you okay?" he asked again.

"Yeah," she said, her mouth drooling a little for the kiss that she hadn't gotten.

"Just a sec." Cannon walked over to where another man was trying to come to a standing position. He placed that black brass knuckle thing against the back of the guy's ribs and said, "You had your chance to walk away."

Snap! went the electricity and the man fell twitching, face down in the sand.

Cannon picked up a couple gadgets and tucked them away, except for the flashlight, which he used to keep an eye on their attackers. So the weapons had been real too. That didn't surprise Daisy; she didn't have the imagination to come up with all those different types of stun devices.

He dialed 9-1-1 and gave a quick and dirty run down of what had happened, then asked for a police and medical response.

Daisy just stared around at the carnage, still having a hard time wrapping her mind around how quickly this had happened. Her hero boyfriend really was like a living, breathing Harry Dresden, just instead of using spells for fire and electricity, he used a veritable arsenal of stun gadgets that she hadn't even known he was carrying.

"What if they'd had guns?" she asked.

He got that amused smile again. "I would have dealt with it." He faced her and she could see concern grow on his face even in the darkness. "I'm sorry if you felt threatened."

"I ... actually no, I didn't feel threatened at all. Even though I didn't know you were a super spy action wizard hero or something, I felt safe. They could've had an army and I would have felt safe."

Cannon took another glance around to make sure no one was going anywhere. Seeing that the scene was secure, he put an arm around her lower back and pulled her close. She could feel his steady breath on her face and her heart kicked into overdrive.

The way he looked at her like some super spy who'd just saved the world made her knees weak. But he was a million times better than some playboy movie spy. He had softness to him in contrast to the hardness she'd just witnessed. Throttling six men one second, and holding her so softly and tenderly the next.

He leaned forward and when their lips touched it was more thrilling than her first time on stage in college singing "I Could Have Danced All Night." It was satin and stone in the perfect combination. Already primed by his studly heroics, she melted into his embrace and into the kiss. She was helpless to resist, even if she had wanted to. His lips were sweet, sweet stun devices and she was glued to where she stood and loving every second of it.

She felt his eyes open and opened hers to see him looking over her shoulder. She turned her head to see a guy trying to crawl away. The stun baton was suddenly in Cannon's hand and extended at full length. He didn't even have to move to reach out to him and give him a prod like a naughty cow would get.

Yet another guy went into the sand twitching like a daddy long-legs spider's amputated leg.

He looked back at her and said, "No mind switch that time."

Daisy giggled, amazed he was so good at seeing that.

A pair of flashlights announced two cops coming down the sand toward them. Cannon stepped away from Daisy half a step and held his arms out. His posture was super natural and unthreatening; it was hard to imagine he was responsible for the scene around them.

"I have two firearms," he announced calmly. "One ankle holster, one belt."

The cops visibly tensed, and one drew his weapon but kept it pointed at the sand. Cannon remained calm and unthreatening.

He'd had guns the whole time! Why hadn't he used them? That was easy for Daisy to answer: he hadn't needed them. So many men would have started with the guns instead of trying to talk their way out of a confrontation, then ending it with the minimal amount of effective force. His hero status bumped up a few notches.

"Any other weapons?" asked one of the cops.

"A stun baton, blast knuckles stun gun, a stun gun flashlight, a pocketknife, a straightblade knife, kick spikes in the laces of my right shoe," he looked at Daisy and gave her a sly smile, "and my fists."

A short cackle escaped Daisy's mouth, but the officer was not amused. "I recommend you don't try being funny. You preparing for the zombie apocalypse?"

With a straight face, he replied, "Not being funny, but I don't think electricity affects zombies."

"You're probably right. So why are you walking around pimped out like a one-man army?" He held the flashlight on Cannon while his partner pulled Cannon's guns.

A couple more flashlights approached with policemen behind them.

"I work in personal security," said Cannon. "My concealed carry permit is in my wallet."

The cop grabbed that as well.

"Ma'am, are you carrying?"

"Me?" asked Daisy. "No. Uh uh."

A couple of the men stood and tried sneaking away but the cops ordered them to a stop.

Cannon said, "These men attacked us. I was defending myself and the lady."

When the other cops arrived, they put handcuffs on everyone, Cannon and Daisy included. Then they separated them to ask them all questions separately.

More police came, as well as some paramedics to take a look at the injured guys. After the interviews, the cops conferred and it didn't take long to decide that Cannon and Daisy were telling the truth and the other guys had started everything. They dropped the handcuffs, took Cannon and Daisy's contact info, and gave Cannon his guns back.

Cannon and Daisy thanked them and walked back toward the restaurant.

"Sorry about that," said Cannon. "Are you sure you're okay?"

"How could I be wrong with you here with me?"

"Not how you wanted to spend your date, though. Do you need to go? Have I put you off or scared you away?"

Anything but. She could tell he was giving her an out but she didn't want it. "It's late, but I don't have anywhere to be."

"Let's head back to my car. Drive to somewhere more populated and talk more." He took her hand, and she wondered if he had residual electricity coursing through him because she could feel the zing.

"That was amazing, Cannon. You realize that?"

"I know," he agreed heartily. "Best kiss I've ever had."

She laughed. "I wasn't talking about the kiss, even though it was amazing too."

Cannon shrugged. "Six drunk guys? Not really."

"My ex-fiancé would've run away screaming."

She felt a hitch in his step. "Fiancé?" He let her hand go and put an arm around her.

If she knew it would get that reaction she would have told him about Sterling sooner. "We dated for three years, all through his internship and residency."

"A doctor?" Cannon's voice rose a little. He was actually flustered already by the conversation, which made Daisy feel a little bit special. "What happened."

"Remember what I told you about not being second place in a man's eyes? That I wanted you to not be distracted tonight?"

"Yeah. Did I pass?"

"First things first," she told him. "Sterling didn't pass. There was always something more important than me."

"Well he's an idiot."

Daisy laughed again. "But you passed. So far. Even before saving my life, you had passed."

They arrived at a black Land Rover with tinted windows, the kind of car she expected to see in a presidential motorcade. He opened the door for her, but before she could climb in, he stole another little kiss. Hopefully there was more of that coming tonight from her probably boyfriend.

The inside of the car was like a spy car—large console, a walkie-talkie type radio, extra buttons and knobs that she was afraid to touch because she didn't want to launch a missile or eject herself.

Cannon climbed in and when he put the key in, the spy dashboard really came to life.

"Nice ride," she said.

"Company car," replied Cannon. "I tricked up the inside a little bit."

"You and your gadgets."

The metal bracelet he wore on his wrist started buzzing and a pale blue LED started running around it. Before she could ask if that was connected to the car, Cannon had his phone in his hand, hit a couple of buttons and held it to his ear.

"This is Culver. Tango seven seven."

Daisy couldn't hear whoever was on the other end of the line.

"I'm fine. The police had my phone for minute."

"No, I'm clear."

He listened for a minute.

"Uh huh. Right away." He hung up and started the car. "Daisy, I have to run."

Just like that? "So our date's over? No drive? No talking more?" She shook her head and exhaled sharply. "Wasn't I *just* talking about being dumped or neglected over and over?"

"I'm sorry, Daisy. My brother's in trouble."

"Warsong?"

"No, my ... one of my other brothers. I really don't have time to explain. Which way's your house?"

Other brother? He'd said earlier he had one brother and one sister. "I can come along," said Daisy. "This date hasn't been exciting enough for me yet, I'm down for another emergency."

He jerked out a laugh. "I thought you'd be terrified by now."

"Not with you by my side," she said, not joking in the slightest.

His mood changed momentarily, then he was antsy again. "Your house? Unless you'd rather catch an Uber, I can call one for you."

"You're so romantic," she said with a little bite. She pointed to the right. What was happening? Hadn't she *just* finished telling him how much she hated to be pushed to the side? Everything was perfect until things had fallen off a cliff. "Is the mission life or death, Cannon?"

He was driving fast and they'd already reached the next turn so she pointed to the left.

"It's not a mission, I mean anything you could really help with."

So it wasn't life or death or he would have told her. So why did he have to drop her like a hot rock? What was it about her that made her always second fiddle in the eyes of everyone she cared about?

Two turns later, they had pulled up in front of her house. Cannon hopped out to open her door and walk her up to her house.

"This really is an emergency," he said. "I wouldn't do this to you otherwise."

Daisy sighed. That was probably true, but how often would emergencies come up? "It always is." He didn't have time, or interest, to listen to her sob story about her dating history, so she added, "Thanks for dinner. And protecting me. I still can't believe not a single one of them touched you."

He shrugged off the compliment. "It was kind of my fault they came after us. Maybe I shouldn't have asked him to shut up in the restaurant. Thanks for being such a good sport about it." At her front door, he turned to her. "I really had a great a great time, Daisy. I'd like to take you out again."

Just like at the restaurant, she was the focus of his life right now, but she knew that in a few seconds he would be running off to take care of something more important.

"I had fun too," she said. "And thanks for … standing up for me." That was something no man had done for her, and very few men even could to the degree that Cannon had done. She opened her arms for a hug, but Cannon came in fast and took her face in his hands, then took command of her lips just like he'd taken charge of the fight earlier.

Daisy wrapped her arms around his large shoulders, surprised again at the bulk that his clothes always downplayed.

The kiss was simple, but there was no doubt he meant it, their lips locking into place, then taking slight maneuvers to explore the surface and spark electricity over the entirety of their lips. She could still taste a hint of sweet chocolate mixed with the mint he'd had on the way out of the restaurant.

"Mmm," she said as he released her, then giggled at herself. Well, at least she hadn't zoned out again.

"I'll call you," he said, taking a step back.

The date was officially over, and it was a good thing he hadn't asked her out again right then and there because he had weakened her defenses with that kiss. Daisy was too confused to commit to anything right away; she needed a little time for some serious reflection. He was waiting for something. Oh, he wouldn't leave until she was safe inside.

"Be safe," she said, though why she didn't know. It was anyone but him that had to worry because nothing could ever hurt this man.

After all, she was plain Jane, and he was an action-hero ninja who was used to hanging out with billionaires and the Queen of England's personal artist.

Be safe, she told herself as she went inside. *Protect that heart of yours, girl.*

CANNON CLIMBED into his SUV and gunned it, driving as fast as was safe on this residential road.

What a date that had been, unlike anything he'd ever experienced. Daisy helped him stay on the surface of life where things were good, and life was happy. Yeah, he had opened up about some of the deeper stuff, but even that hadn't been dark like sometimes in the past.

Daisy Close was exactly what he needed in his life. Right then and there he made the decision to take any steps necessary to win her over.

Yet here he was, rushing off to bow to Sutton and help a brother, leaving her in the dust. But what was he supposed to do? Zane needed him, and this was just a date, the first of many dates with her.

Even as he said that, he knew it was wrong. That had been more than just a date, and Daisy was more than just a woman. She was the woman he wanted in his life forever. He couldn't wait to see her again, to put his arms around her, feel the softness of her and draw on her strength and goodness. To hold her hand, to see that gorgeous dimple when she smiled. To have her look at him again like *she* was *his* rock.

He could tell she wasn't happy when he'd ended their date. But it had been mostly over already, hadn't it?

Now he was just making excuses. What would Zane have said back in the Philippines if Cannon had tried pulling out these weak excuses? He would have told him, jokingly, that if he wanted to make excuses, he should have chosen the Air Force.

Throughout BUD/S and SEAL training, Cannon had never once opened his mouth to make an excuse, so what was up now? He was conflicted, that was it. Did his loyalties lie with his brothers, who he'd trained with, fought with, bled for, and always been there for? Or did he owe a woman he just barely met who wasn't having a major emergency his loyalty?

The answer was obvious, right?

Right?

Never had he let a brother down. Never had he let the team down. Not SEAL Team 7, and not anyone in the Warrior Project.

So why did his gut keeping telling him he was wrong?

Zane had a true emergency or else he wouldn't have used the Coms band, so why was Cannon still worrying about something he could do nothing about right now?

Maybe that wasn't right. Maybe he could do something. He ordered his car to send a text to Daisy: *Sorry for running off. I'll give you details later. Hope you give me another chance.*

She sent back a winking emoji and: *If you're lucky.*

That had to be good enough for now.

Distractions had never caused problems for Cannon, but he seriously wondered if he'd be able to focus on the job tonight.

10

The day after their date, Daisy got a text from Cannon. It was good to know he was safe after whatever emergency he'd had to deal with, but after sleeping on it, she felt more than ever that she needed a guy who was going to be devoted to her. She'd come so close to throwing her life away as Sterling's trophy wife, she couldn't let that happen again.

Still, she couldn't stop thinking about how exciting it was to go out with Cannon. Even before the fight, it was a thrill to spend one-on-one time with him. Then when danger came, he hadn't even batted an eye.

She still couldn't figure out if he was James Bond, or Harry Dresden, or maybe even Dr. Strange with the way he seemed to be under completely different time constraints than the guys he had fought. Someday they'd make a movie about this peaceful man with a dangerous side once he got pushed too far.

Just thinking about him made her heart race. She wanted him so bad, but she wanted the version of him who made her feel important *all* of the time. Or at least *most* of the time. Every encounter they'd had so far, he'd been distracted or called away. She was so torn.

Not that she was ready to give up on Cannon, but she would proceed with caution.

So she turned down his request for a date, even though she really wanted to go. Maybe not being at his beck and call would help him figure out his priorities.

The next day, Wednesday morning, Daisy had an idea. She picked up her phone and dialed Cannon.

"Culver," he said after one ring.

"Hey, Culver," she said in a serious tone. "It's Close."

He chuckled. "Hi, Close."

"You knew it was me before you answered," she told him, "so why all military seriousness still?"

"Habit," he said. "Next time I'll ... I don't know. How do normal people answer the phone?"

"In the U.S.? Hello usually works."

"Hello," he said, trying out the word. "I'll give it a shot."

"Wanna go on a date?" She was too excited to wait any longer.

"I thought you'd never ask. Just say when and where."

"I'm up for an award from the North American Literary Society—"

"What! That's amazing! I mean, it sounds amazing, why didn't you mention it like first thing when we met?"

"You mean, like, 'Hi, I'm Daisy, I've been nominated for a semi-major award'?"

"That's what I would do," he said.

"I'll think about it," she told him. "Anyway, I'm a longshot for the award, but there's a fancy banquet and all that. What do you think?" The thought of seeing Cannon in a tux on the red carpet almost made Daisy zone off in a little fantasy. Oh wait, no red carpet, but the tux could be a real thing.

"I am so in," he said. "When is it?"

The excitement in his voice made Daisy feel all energetic and excited for the date.

"No running off? No being distracted?"

"Cross my heart, hope to die," he said. "Just tell me when it is and what to wear."

"It's a week from Saturday."

"Oh no. Saturday?"

"Yeah, next Saturday night."

Cannon groaned. "I work Saturday. I'm on a train every Saturday, either northbound or southbound. And even if I'm southbound, the train is delayed more often than not, so there's no guarantee I could make it after the train ride."

That's right. Daisy should have known that, but she still felt totally bummed out after getting her hopes up and picturing him in his fancy tux. And once again she was back to the same question: would he ever put her first in his life?

"Do you ever get days off?" It wasn't like she was asking him to get it off so they could go see a movie. This was a once-in-a-lifetime event for her.

"No," he said, "except for the five and a half days I'm not working."

"You haven't had a Saturday off since you started working for the Golds?"

Cannon paused. "How'd you know ... I guess the info is out there, even though I never told you Pasha's last name. Anyway, no. The custody arrangement is rock solid, and Mr. ... my employer hand-selected me for the job."

"No one can cover for you? None of your other brothers?"

"No. Our contract is very clear about that. If I don't go, Pasha doesn't go, and then it's custody apocalypse."

That sounded bad. Daisy didn't want to cause any type of apocalypse. "Well, it was worth a shot," she told him. She knew she had failed to keep her disappointment out of her voice. Actually she hadn't tried to keep the disappointment from being apparent.

"Are you free tonight? Tomorrow? Sunday? Monday? Not that I'm desperate or anything, but ... well, yeah, I'm dying to see you."

Daisy understood he had to work, and she could work with his schedule, but every time she gave him a chance, it went perfect for a while then took a nosedive. She couldn't just keep letting that happen. "How do I know I won't get dumped halfway through the date?"

Cannon didn't answer. A veritable eternity passed over about fifteen seconds.

"Cannon? Did I lose you?"

"I'm still here."

Wow, even after begging to go out with her he couldn't make a simple promise to complete one single date. Her excitement had transformed into disappointment, and was starting to rise into frustration.

"Let's take it slow," she said. "I'll give you some time to figure out if you want to date me or date your job and your brothers."

"Daisy—"

"I can take your Friday, Saturday schedule. I don't expect you to quit your job for me after one date—well, half a date. But I won't be a back-up option. I can't hang around on the sidelines just in case you decide you have a little time for me."

"Daisy, please—"

"I'm not mad, Cannon, and I'm not saying we're through, but you can't even commit to one single uninterrupted date, and I am *not* doormat material."

"What can I do?" he said pleadingly.

"I've told you what I want, what I *need* from a boyfriend. Just like in my editing work, it's not my job to tell you how to fix it. Give me a call in a few days if you figure it out."

With a trembling thumb, she ended the call. Just then tears

spilled over and ran down both sides of her face. She was nervous and disappointed, but mostly proud of herself. Doormat might have been a little overstated, but at the moment that was how she felt. Tough as it was, she knew she had to stand her ground now to give them both the best chance at a happily ever after.

CANNON STARED AT HIS SCREEN. Sure enough, she'd hung up on him.

Doormat? Had he really made her feel like a doormat?

He wanted to throw up. Without taking time to consider, he dialed Daisy's number.

Voicemail. He dialed again, and voicemail again.

For two nights now he'd lost sleep because he knew that he might not have a shot with her if he couldn't figure out how to balance dating with his responsibilities, but finding out that he had hurt her that badly made him physically ill. What was the purpose of anything in his life if he made the woman he cared about so much feel like a doormat?

Oh man, he really was going to throw up.

Since calling wasn't working, he tried texting. *Daisy, I am so so so sorry I made you feel like that. I know I have a lot to learn about dating. I'm going to figure this out. Please give me another chance.*

Why couldn't this be simple? Like a fight. Man against man, strength and preparation and the grace of God deciding the victor.

His phone dinged. *Figure it out. Then let me know.*

At least that was something. Too bad Cannon had no idea where to start.

HOURS AFTER DAISY had hung up on him, Cannon felt a little better. He didn't have a plan exactly, but he had a next step. As he drove down the familiar I-5 from Los Angeles to San Diego, he used the voice features of his SUV to order roses to be delivered to Daisy's house. It would have been better to have them delivered to a public place like her job, but since she had a home office, he didn't have a choice.

He wanted to text, he wanted to call, he wanted to show up on her doorstep, but he still hadn't figured anything out. Hopefully his next move would give him some idea of how to fix things with her.

Why he had chosen Sutton Smith to talk to about his women problems, he didn't know. Corbin had a little experience, but he hadn't come back to Earth from the honeymoon phase yet. None of the other SEALs had any experience with women to speak of, except River who was up a serious creek in regards to some duke's daughter. As far as Cannon knew, Sutton and River were in the planning stages of some grand rescue in England.

At least Sutton had been married at one point, to Doug's mother. But that had only lasted long enough for Doug to be born, then it had been Sutton and Doug on their own. Who else did Cannon have to turn to? His years in the military had been enough to split all the close ties with Warsong and Pike and his parents had died years ago from smoking-related cancers.

Traffic was relatively light and he pulled up to Sutton's place in record time. He loved coming here. Architecture wasn't Cannon's strong point, but he'd heard English Tudor thrown around in regards to the humongous mansion with all the peaks in the roof and expansive floors. It featured upgraded everything and sat on a few acres right on an ocean cliff. It was one of the premier properties in Southern California.

Besides, it always felt like coming home. Even though his home as a child was inner city ghetto and nothing like this upscale way of life, it was still home. While Cannon had never been in love with money, or craved the lifestyle of this type of house, it was satisfying to be able to walk through the front doors without knocking and make himself at home. Doug had grown up here, and Cannon could still feel a little bit of him here.

He pulled up behind the twin of his SUV. Probably River's vehicle. The front of the property was aged red brick in various geometric configurations with half a dozen steps leading to the front door. There was stone accent here and there, mostly on the foundation as if this was a new style of British castle. Cannon pushed open the huge front door and nodded at the security guy sitting in the lobby. In addition to the SEALs in the Warrior Project, Sutton had a whole team of private security guys. Ever since River had started stirring up trouble with that duke back in England, the mansion had been on high alert. Maybe not DEFCON 5, but at least DEFCON 3.

Agatha appeared in the lavish entry way and hurried over to him in her way of taking quick, short steps. "Oh, Cannon, my boy. It's so good to see ya."

She was dressed in her usual bright garb. Today it was a purple blouse with loose orange and pink swirled leggings. The loud outfit made her white hair seem like part of the get-up but it was her real hair. Agatha had been taking care of Sutton since he was a child, and seemed to enjoy the chance to mother the SEALs who came through his house.

"Hi, Agather," he told her, mimicking her accent. He gave her a hug and a kiss on the cheek.

"You boys like to have your fun, but one of these days we'll have you in jolly ol' England and we'll see then who talks funny. Now, can I get you something to eat?"

"No thanks. I need to talk to Sutton. Is he around?" Let her think that they had some important security business to talk about. If she found out he was looking for advice about girls, he'd never hear the end of it.

"I'll take you back," said River, coming around the corner into the entryway. A guy Cannon didn't know trailed in with River.

Agatha said, "I'll leave you to it, then. Don't you forget to say cheerio before you leave, Cannon."

"If you're near the ice cream counter, I won't be able to miss you," he said as she walked away. He clasped hands with River and pulled him in for a one-arm man-hug. Worry and stress were obvious on River's face. Cannon hadn't seen him looking so worn-down since their SEAL days.

"You hanging in there?" asked Cannon.

"I guess. What choice do I have? How about you, Barney? How's the babysitting?"

Cannon laughed. Oh, it was good to have brothers, even in hard times. "Life is good, man. I'm still getting paid the big bucks to ride trains, play Candyland, and watch Disney movies."

"That sounds perfect for you, choir boy." River wasn't smiling but there was a certain timbre to a man's voice when he was messing with you.

"Yeah, way too plebeian for a silk-stocking aristocrat like you."

River chuckled. "Hey, this is Steve."

The new guy stepped up. He had a young-looking face, mid-twenties, with white-blond hair. They shook hands, both gripping a little harder than they had to.

Cannon could recognize a new SEAL that Sutton had taken in to help with the transition to normal life. "What Team were you?"

"The best one," said Steve. "Team 6."

Cannon feigned confusion. "They must not have taught you how to count in your training because if you're talking about the best, you mean 7."

"A West Coast team?" replied Steve with the same fake surprise. "Surfer dudes and muscle heads? If you think 7 is the best, you must've been concussed one time too many."

"Careful," said River playfully. "Them's fighting words around here. The founding Warrior Project guys are all Team 7."

"Ah," said Steve, suddenly understanding. "*That* explains why they brought me in. To fix the place up."

Cannon and River chuckled. Steve would fit right in around here.

"Welcome aboard," said Cannon. "If you need anything, I've got a good listening ear."

River said, "He's a former Navy Chaplain and still our informal therapist, pastor, and conscience. Feel free to confess all your sins. He'll even give you a sticker that says, *Forgiven*.

It was so good to be back with the guys, even when they gave him a hard time. He told Steve, "Hopefully someone warned you not to listen to a thing River says. But seriously, I'll listen if you need to talk."

"Thanks, brother." They shook hands and did the man-hug. "I'll let you guys catch up." Steve walked out, leaving them alone in the huge entryway.

River spoke in a quiet tone. "Hey, the plan we talked about? The mission in England? It's looking like a go. Sutton'll brief you when we get closer, but I have a favor to ask."

"Anything, man. Unless you want to borrow one of my pistols. Or my dart gun, stun baton, volt shockers, or … well pretty much, you can't play with my toys."

Some of the stress on River's face faded as he smiled. "You perform weddings, right?"

"I've done a few."

"How do you feel about becoming ordained in the U.K.?"

Now that did sound fun. "I'm in. Just tell me when and where and I'll be there with my stole on."

"I knew I could count on you."

"Who am I marrying?" asked Cannon.

With a conspiratorial chuckle, River put an arm around Cannon and led him away while he filled him in on the details.

Even the hallway was something out of a movie set with large wood beams framing it every six feet or so. When they reached the doorway to Sutton's huge office, River stopped and said, "I'm glad I can count on you, Big Gun."

"Any time, man." He'd always been there for the other guys and had never had trouble telling them that before, but now he wondered if he really could be there for them all the time. Life was suddenly complicated. It was what he'd come to talk to Sutton about.

River left and Cannon felt relieved that he was past the small talk and could get to business with Sutton. He walked across the huge room to where Sutton sat at a desk with papers, maps, and house plans spread out over it. The room was the size of Cannon's apartment and the million-dollar views were worth more than Cannon would make in a lifetime.

"Is all that for River's top secret mission?"

"Aye," said Sutton, finally looking up. "We've been at it all morning. Good timing, because he needed a break." Sutton was in his late 40s, and still had the bearing of an admiral, but the body of a front-line Special Ops soldier. He also still had most of his British accent. Cannon always felt like he was talking to a truly experienced James Bond-type when he talked to Sutton.

"I know things are crazy," said Cannon as he sat in the chair across the desk. "Thanks for taking some time."

"Everything fine with Miss Gold?"

"Perfect," said Cannon. "It's Miss Close I can't figure out."

Sutton leaned back in his chair, finally understanding what was so urgent, and apparently amused by it. "She's the young lady you met on the train."

"Yes, sir."

"And why do you think I know the first thing about women?" His eyes went to the desk and one hand absentmindedly covered a photo, but not before Cannon saw that it was that beautiful British Lady who was always on the red carpet. Liz ... Gunthry? She was often called the most beautiful woman alive or something like that, but Cannon never paid attention to British royalty or celebrities in general. "Maybe I should get Agatha in here."

"No!" said Cannon. "Let's keep this between us men."

Sutton sat up and studied Cannon. "You're the one the guys go to when they need some guidance. You tell them how to fix their problems."

"I don't tell them," said Cannon, and it was true. "They talk about it and figure it out themselves."

"All you do is listen? A broken telephone box could do that."

"All right," said Cannon. "Sometimes I throw out one or two carefully crafted questions and maybe a scripture if I'm feeling pious that day."

"I know even less about women than I do about American Football, but if you're fine with me using your technique against you, let's give her a try."

Sutton wasn't one for long, redundant stories, so Cannon described their relationship as briefly as possible, up to the texts about figuring out his priorities. Sutton tented his fingers and rested them over his jaw. A full minute passed before he said, "You bring this up at an ... interesting time, and I can't help but wonder about the timing." He paused and looked out the window at the ocean for a bit. Still not looking at Cannon, he said, "I lost the woman I loved because I put something else before her."

That was news to Cannon. "The Royal Navy? Your career?"

Sutton nodded, still gazing out over the ocean. "I'd trade it all."

Cannon was too stunned to speak for a while. "Are you telling me—"

"That's not how it works," interrupted Sutton. "I'm only supposed to ask short questions, possibly biblical in nature. Not tell you anything. So, isn't there something about putting off childish things?"

If Sutton didn't know there was, he wouldn't have asked. "It's in

Corinthians," said Cannon. *"When I was a child, I spoke as a child, I understood as a child, I thought as a child, but when I became a man, I put away childish things."*

Sutton nodded. "Are you ready to be a man?"

"What? Because I'm doing my duty and being loyal to my fellow SEALs?"

Sutton's eyebrows rose again, as if Cannon had answered his own question, but he still had no idea what Sutton was trying to tell him.

Since Sutton wasn't going to explain, Cannon said, "I know the British Royal Navy isn't quite the SEALs, but you know we are considered men among boys wherever we go. A SEAL is the pinnacle of manliness. Nothing against Her Majesty's fleet or its sailors, but when I gave up being a Navy Chaplain to become a Navy SEAL, that's when I became a man."

"Is that so?"

"Yes," said Cannon confidently. "That's when I put off childish things." No child could go through the training he'd received. No child could experience what Cannon and the others went through in the Philippines, Iraq, Somalia, Afghanistan.

Sutton just nodded slightly and bored into Cannon with his eyes. Is this how the other guys saw Cannon when he tried to listen to their problems and guide them to answers? Because if it was, Cannon needed a new hobby.

Either way, Sutton was telling him to be a man. But how did that help him know how to proceed with Daisy when the manly thing to do was to have his brother's backs and worry about other people's security before he worried about what he wanted, like spending time with Daisy?

Oh, this was such a tough principle to crack. Cannon asked, "Why would God make it so hard to chose between making myself and Daisy happy, and doing my duty as a loyal friend and brother?"

"Why would he make it easy?" exclaimed Sutton. "Who was the bloke in the Bible who had to work a dozen years to get his wife."

"Jacob," said Cannon. "Fourteen years." Cannon would rather go through Hell Week again rather than wait fourteen years for Daisy.

"What about when Eve bit the apple? Did Adam have an easy decision? Blimey, he had to choose between his wife and God."

"So that's all you have for me? It won't be easy?"

Sutton went on to say, "I'm no pastor, but I've had my wrestles with God over the years, and not *once* has it been easy." He glanced down to where that photo was hidden and muttered, "And not once have I won when it really mattered."

Was that a gleam of tears in Sutton's eyes? Impossible. The man didn't know the meaning of the word cry. As far as Cannon knew, he didn't have tear glands.

"But do I give up?" Sutton's question was low and a little bitter.

Of course he didn't give up, he was Sutton Smith. Quit was another word that wasn't in his vocabulary.

With a clenched jaw, Sutton's face rose toward Cannon. An answer was coming. Wisdom was about to be dispensed.

"Are you going to give up, Cannon?"

"Never. I've never given up on anything worthy."

"I believe that," said Sutton. "None of you men would give up. So my question is, does Miss Close know that?"

"That I'll never give up? Of course she does. She knows I'm a SEAL, she knows ..." What did she know? Why did Cannon think he had any idea what she knew?

"Cannon." Sutton was staring intensely at Cannon, his blue eyes like icicles. "If you offered to trade me another chance with the woman I loved, I would sign over every one of my possessions before you even finished speaking. Now, how much would you sacrifice for Miss Close?"

"Everything."

"Everything?" asked Sutton. "So easy for a young man to say that. Not so easy to live it."

"I would give anything," objected Cannon. "Everything. I feel like I can't live without her. I ... she ..." He didn't want to go into the darkness of his past and how she helped him focus on the light.

They looked at each other for a minute. What else could Cannon say? What else could he accomplish here?

"Thanks, Sutton." They hadn't really decided or discovered anything. Cannon already knew he was crazy about Daisy. Now he needed to go figure out what to do about it.

"I hope the Good Lord gives you more success than he's given me when it comes to women."

"Me too," said Cannon.

"I'll be in touch," said Sutton. "Preliminary schedule for River's mission is next Thursday through Saturday. I will make the arrangements with Mr. Gold if there is a timeline conflict, because we need you on this one."

Wow, the mission was that important? That reminded Cannon that he had some work to do if he wanted to be ordained in the U.K. by then.

"Cheers," said Cannon, standing.

"Cheers," said Sutton. "Heart of a warrior." He went back to work.

"Heart of a warrior," muttered Cannon as he walked away. Even that made Cannon remember Daisy's reaction to his book blurb comment.

So what now? Maybe something would come to mind if he let it incubate.

The house was huge but right in the center of everything was an eight-flavor ice cream counter. Even if Cannon didn't have great situational awareness of the premises, he'd know the ice cream bar was central because it never took him long to get there. Some of the SEALs loved the indoor lap pool or bowling alley, some of the guys liked the huge grounds where you could run a marathon in about three laps, and they all loved to grab some ropes and climb on the cliff face over the ocean. But of all the amenities of this unreal mansion, Cannon's favorite was the ice cream counter.

He took a waffle cone from the huge glass jar and started scooping double chocolate malted crunch.

Agatha approached on the far side of the counter and bent her head to look into his eyes. He knew that somehow Agatha would know this hadn't been a professional visit.

"Did you get the answers you came for, love?"

Cannon stopped scooping and his eyes unfocused for a bit. "I got more questions."

"Maybe that's for the best," she told him. "Maybe you weren't asking the right questions t' begin with."

Cannon finished filling the cone.

What would I give up for Daisy? Does she know I won't give up on her? Cannon knew he was as ignorant about women as, well, a broken telephone box, but one thing he did know, he would never give up on Daisy.

How do I make her know that?

He wasn't a quitter. Never had been, never would be. Even during BUD/S, even during Hell Week—

"Agather, yer a genius, ya are!" He hustled from the room, before she could reach out and swat him.

He had an idea and wanted to give it a try ASAP.

DAISY STARED at the words on the computer screen, only seeing lines of gibberish against a white background. The manuscript wasn't working, but Daisy couldn't put her finger on the reason why. It wasn't her job to fix the problem, but she had to be able to point to what wasn't working. And though she wrangled this one up and down, she couldn't get to the heart of it.

It was the motivations of the protagonist that just—

A knock came at the door, hard and demanding. Why not ring the doorbell? A delivery? Sometimes UPS and FEDex guys would pound like that then jog back to their truck.

It had only been half a day since the conversation with Cannon. Maybe he was here to make up in person. Hopefully not, because she was in her editor's clothes—pajama shorts and a tank top—and the only attention her hair had received all day was the scrunchie holding it out of her face.

She peeked through the side light and realized it was nighttime. Flipping on the light, she didn't see anyone standing there.

Could it be doorbell ditchers? There were kids in her neighborhood but she hadn't been a target of them before.

Keeping the door chain attached, she cracked the door. Sitting on the center of her welcome mat was a pretty brass bell, but there was no person in sight. The handle was ornate, almost crown-like and the bowl was plain and polished. A rolled up piece of paper was tied to the base of the handle.

Daisy closed the door, undid the chain, then opened it and picked up the bell. The street in front of her house was still quiet.

Inside, she looked at the bell more closely but nothing else stood out to her. She gave a little twist of her wrist, and was disappointed when the bell remained silent. Turning the bell upside down, she saw that it had no clapper. What good was a bell that you couldn't ring?

Hoping the note would elaborate, she opened it, and saw her name followed by a couple of block-style paragraphs.

Daisy,

A bell hangs on the wall at BUD/S training. When a SEAL candidate decides to quit, he rings the bell and that's it. He gets a hot cup of coffee, a warm meal, and a long nap, but he's out. During Hell Week, they bring the bell right down to the beach so you don't even have to run back to camp. I saw that bell every day of training. So many times I thought about how easy it would be to ring it. But then I thought about what I would lose if I rang it.

IN MY RELATIONSHIP WITH YOU, there is no bell. I may struggle, I may fall and do a face plant in the mud, and I may make a fool of myself sitting in the metaphorical surf, shivering in my metaphorical underwear ... but I will never ring the bell. I will never give up. I'll go without food, sleep, and the comforts of life if I have to for you, but I will never give up. You are my new Team. I could never live with knowing what I would lose.

DAISY TURNED the bell upside down and stared into the empty bowl. No, it wasn't a bell, not as far as she was concerned. You could ring a bell, but this was unringable. This was a symbol.

Her nearly boyfriend had been so reticent about the details of his SEAL days, but she'd known that it was a tumultuous layer under his happy exterior. And he'd chosen today, when she had pushed him up against the ropes, to open up to her to compare their relationship with the greatest accomplishment of his life. She was his Team. Did that mean she was his priority? If it didn't mean that now, she had faith that he'd figure it out.

He flat out said he'd never give up.

At this point in their relationship, she couldn't ask for much more. It was a huge step and she had to blink happy tears away.

She texted, *Thanks. I think you're figuring it out.* She sent the text, knowing that he couldn't be more than a few blocks away, if that far.

A response arrived. *Give me a chance tomorrow night?*

Tomorrow would be Thursday. If she didn't see him then, she'd have to wait three more days.

Sounds fun! What do you have in mind?

A minute later he replied, *Karaoke? It would be worth letting you hear me sing to be able to hear your voice. Again.*

Yes!

Pick you up at 6. Dinner and singing.

Daisy started waltzing through her house, singing "Unchained Melody." She was going to hear him sing.

DAISY PUSHED her plate with the pizza crusts away and leaned forward on the table, watching Cannon walk up to the short stage at the back of the restaurant. She'd dared him to go first and he hadn't hesitated. He wasn't moving with his normal confidence, but there he was picking up the mic.

The familiar piano music that instantly reminded her of *Toy Story* started up, and Cannon gave her a wink.

"*You got a friend in me,*" he sang, smiling like always. His voice wasn't going to get him to Broadway, but it was so charming and homey. Daisy felt a little stab of jealousy for Pasha, who got to hear him sing every week. There was no goofiness to Cannon's singing, like the original version of this song, just her singing boyfriend, up on stage in front of the whole world just because she had dared him to go.

It made her feel all warm inside.

When he finished, Daisy whooped and clapped so energetically the rest of the place joined in. He came back and practically collapsed into the chair next to her.

"Not bad for your first time ever singing in public," she told him, giving him a high five.

"Oh no," he told her, and she noticed his special amused smile. "I deserve more than a hand slap for going up there."

Daisy loved that idea, and leaned in so he could kiss her. It was just a peck, but once again, she felt like the only thing in the world as far as he was concerned. This night had started out good and gotten even better.

"I still don't know how you got me to go up there," he said, picking up his water and chugging some.

"Look at you all flustered and nervous." She actually loved seeing him like this. Any time she chose she could think back to how he'd been the manliest man ever in that fight on the beach, so it was kind of fun to see him vulnerable.

Up until the time to sing he'd been so relaxed and yet focused on her and everything had been perfect all evening. Of course, no one could call him because he'd left his phone in the car so he wouldn't be distracted. As long as that metal band he wore on his wrist didn't light up, she was pretty sure she'd have him for the rest of the night.

"You want any more food or dessert?" he asked.

"Nah." The wood-fired pizza was delicious, but she'd had plenty. "I'm good just enjoying the ambiance." With him being her focused boyfriend, she could just chill almost anywhere and be happy.

"You have to get up there and sing," he told her. "Come on, that lady's almost done."

"Go with me," she said, expecting him to flat out refuse.

"Duet?"

"Yes!" Was he really going to do it? For her? "Please!"

He shrugged one shoulder. "All right."

They went up to the DJ as "Don't Stop Believing" wrapped up and Daisy picked "I Got You, Babe."

The song started with Daisy singing, and went back and forth. During the chorus they harmonized automatically and somehow his slightly gritty voice blended nicely with her more cultured voice.

Being on stage with him, singing this love song in front of a couple dozen people was a new and exciting experience for her, and she wanted it to last forever. When Cannon sang the line, "*I got you to wear my ring,*" he gave her a wink that knocked her off balance and made her miss the first few words of her line.

The song ended and they went back to their booth. "Not too bad," she told him, with a smile.

"With you up there, how could it not be great?" he countered. "You really are amazing."

"I should be," she said. "I had voice lessons for ten years."

"I'm not talking about singing," he said, focused on her with laser intensity. "Just being with you changes everything in my world. I wish I didn't have to get on a train tomorrow morning. I wish I could just spend the whole weekend with you."

Daisy's whole body tingled, partly from the thrill of sharing that experience with him but mostly because he'd said exactly what she was feeling. This date had been simple and perfect, so far, and if she could get a couple more of those types of dates then she'd really know that he cared enough about her to put her first when they were together.

"You better get some sleep tonight," she told him, still a little afraid to get too deep into the relationship discussion. "We should go."

His back straightened almost imperceptibly. "I'm not leaving until I hear you sing. Without me."

"Fine," she said, loving how firm he was about it. "But we'll have to wait a few songs so people don't get sick of us."

He put an arm around her and she leaned back against him and got comfortable with her head on his shoulder and her back against his strong chest and abs. She was in no hurry.

After a few songs, an opening came up so she hurried to the front and sang, "Unchained Melody," thinking the whole time about that first night on the train and their long whispered conversation.

As she sang, she couldn't deny the feeling that she honestly couldn't help falling in love with him.

When she came back to the booth, he was standing up and clapping, not trying to involve the whole place in the applause, but clapping only for her. He wrapped her up, picked her off her feet as easy as if she was made of feathers, and gave her a delicious kiss that she felt all the way down in her toes.

They left the restaurant and he drove her home and walked her to door. She made a half-hearted invitation to come in, and he turned it down. She didn't push because she knew he had to leave for the train early in the morning, and also she didn't want him to get the wrong idea about what exactly she was inviting him to.

But he did kiss her, the best one yet. And as he kissed her she imagined them standing on a rock outcropping at the beach, with waves crashing around them, her and him alone, deeply into the kiss, and savoring every second of it. If she'd had any doubt about his claims of never giving up, she had to believe his kiss.

He left her giddy, wanting more in such a good way.

All night long he had been all hers and it was so perfect. Cannon was definitely figuring it out. No real tests had come, but they would, eventually.

Something was different when she thought about a future with him. In the past whenever she thought of the possibility of being pushed to the side, it stressed her out. The bell without a clapper and the magical date tonight had helped her realize that he was willing to go to lengths and she should too. They both had to make sacrifices for the person they loved. There was a difference between being needy and respecting herself, and Daisy was starting to see the line.

At some point in the future, something would come up and she'd have to let Cannon go, without any resentment or frustration.

The strange thing was ... Daisy thought she could do it. She could meet him in the middle, both leaving their starting places so they could be together on new, better ground.

The thought of that future with him had her too energized to sleep, so she pulled up her laptop to keep going with her current edit, but an idea struck her.

Maybe another trip to Seattle was in order. They really could spend the weekend together. They could be together with him putting Pasha and his job first, and Daisy being perfectly fine with it. She pulled up the Amtrak site to find out if there were any open roomettes.

She just couldn't stand the thought of not seeing him before Sunday, so she texted him, asking if he would mind a tag-along on the train, and promising to let him do his job.

He replied, *I'd never turn down the chance to see your beautiful smile.*

That was good enough for her. She booked it without another thought.

11

Cannon waited outside of Pasha's suite for her and Miss Dee to get settled. There was already something different about this trip, but he couldn't put his finger on it. The crowd on the platform had been like any other—mostly individuals commuting to Central California, older people preparing for a scenic vacation, and a crowd of other people riding for a dozen different reasons. After doing the northbound trip for almost a year now, he figured half of the people on the train would go all the way to Seattle.

What was it about the crowd today that made him nervous? Maybe it wasn't even the crowd. Storm clouds were moving in, and would only get bigger and meaner as they went north. Rain all through Northern California, then snow all through Oregon and Washington. It rarely changed anything with the train or its schedule, but it did give the upcoming security detail an ominous feel.

Of course, he was ignoring the biggest probability. Daisy was here. They'd seen her momentarily on the platform and would be meeting her in a few minutes in the Pacific Parlour car. This would be the third time she'd ridden the train with them, but the first one since they started dating. He had to prove to her that she came first in his life, but how could he do that when Pasha was his one and only priority for the next 36 hours?

Before booking the trip last night, she had texted and asked if he had a problem with it. At the time all he could think was that it meant he could see her and spend time with her.

Now that it was a reality though, he wondered if it had been a mistake because he could not shake this feeling that something was off and he hated the thought that it might be because the woman he'd fallen in love with was on the train. She had promised to let him do his job, so she knew he had to focus on Pasha. Hopefully this trip wouldn't derail his goal to prove that he would put her first.

The door opened a crack and when Miss Dee saw Cannon standing there, she opened it the rest of the way and Pasha came out. The stairs were always the trickiest part of traversing the cars, and he was glad for a competent counterpart like Miss Dee. He led the way up the stairs, and when they all reached the top, Miss Dee took the lead.

Halfway through the next car, they passed Daisy's room. Pasha greeted her as enthusiastically as usual, and invited her to go to the parlour car with them. Daisy agreed and asked if she wanted to learn Rummikub, which Pasha quickly agreed to.

Cannon gave her a smile and a wink as she took her place in the middle of the procession with Pasha, and got a lovely smile back from her. As much as he wanted a hug and a kiss, he was glad she was fine without it.

He took his attention back to his focus on situational awareness.

Lately, every trip started with a walkthrough of the train, like the one that Pasha had found Daisy with the first time. The security aspect had worried Cannon at first, but he had discussed it with Rasmus Gold and Sutton and agreed that it was okay. Cannon used it as a chance to get eyes on the entire train and scope out any possible threats.

Today was definitely different. Something he couldn't put his finger on. It had to be because his ... girlfriend was on the train with them. Was girlfriend the right word? As far as he was concerned it was. But he didn't have time to think about that. Later, when everyone except for him was sleeping, he could think about it all he wanted. Daisy would probably visit him and they could discuss it together.

The sweep of the train was clear, except for that pesky malaise in the bottom of his gut, but until he could put a name to it—besides 'Daisy'—he'd just be vigilant, like normal. That was horrible. He felt bad for wondering if the weird feelings were because of her presence.

They hung out in the parlour car for an hour, with Cannon sitting to the side while Daisy interacted with Pasha and, to a lesser degree, Miss Dee. Lightning lit the clouds and rain pelted the windows. The storm could very well be the cause of his discomfort.

They split up when Pasha went back to her suite for her lessons. They met up again for dinner, then after Pasha put her PJs on, they headed to the theater car. It only took Cannon about ten guesses to figure out they were watching *The Incredibles*. One of these trips she'd realize he was being obtuse on purpose, and the game would end.

Who was Cannon kidding; she probably knew already and kept playing along for his sake.

In the theater room, Pasha and Miss Dee took their normal seats up front while Cannon took his position in the back of the car. Daisy paused, unsure for a minute. With a questioning look, she motioned to the front, asking if that's where Cannon wanted her to go.

He nodded, reluctantly, and she nodded back understanding, shrugging like, *what are ya gonna do?* Cannon was pretty sure they were both rethinking whether it had been a good idea to spend this time together. Still, he loved being able to see her pretty face throughout the day.

The Blu-ray player wouldn't read the disc, so they had to wait for Felix to round up a replacement. Daisy and Pasha chatted in their funny, intelligent way. Daisy was so beautiful and carefree, she just made the world a better place wherever she went. Cannon loved watching this woman he loved interact with this little girl who he loved like his own daughter. After this trip, he'd do whatever he could to make sure he never had to choose between the two.

The movie eventually started, and it was one of the longer animated movies on the rotation. By the time they finished the movie and said goodnight, it was after eleven. Miss Dee got Pasha all ready for bed, then let him know Pasha was ready for him. Other than when he went in to sweep the room at the beginning of the each trip, it was the only time he went into the suite.

"Keep an eye out," he told Miss Dee as he walked past, and sat on the side of Pasha's bunk. Even though he felt like he knew the cause of the nerves, he was still being extra vigilant. He was tempted to forego the goodnight song so he could keep watch, but he was just being silly.

Miss Dee nodded and kept the door cracked, one eye down the hallway, and one hand under the flap of her coat where she kept her .357. Either she had picked up on a weird vibe from the train, or had figured out that Cannon had.

"Whose turn to pick the song?" asked Cannon, tightening the burrito wrap of Pasha's blankets.

"Oh Cannon. Did you forget again? When I go to Daddy's, you pick. When I go to Mommy's, I get to pick."

"Oh good, because I want to sing 'You Got a Friend in Me'."

Pasha smiled. "I love that one."

Cannon sang it, the same song he'd sung the night before. He'd been as nervous as a new guy showing up for his first day with his SEAL platoon last night, but he'd tried not to show it. It paid off when Daisy had whooped and gotten the whole place to clap for him.

When he finished singing, Pasha gave him that cute little, half-toothless smile. "I'd clap, but I don't wanna mess up my burrito blankets."

"Goodnight, Violet," he told her.

"Goodnight, Mr. Incredible."

Miss Dee pulled the door open for him.

"Restroom," he muttered as he walked passed. They didn't need a lot of words to communicate simple things like that. He grabbed his toothbrush, then went to the restroom, knowing that Miss Dee would have her hand on the butt of her gun and a shoulder against the door until Cannon came back and let her know that he was back on duty.

In the tiny bathroom he put toothpaste on the toothbrush and splashed some water on it. As he lifted the brush to his mouth, he felt or ... sensed something from outside.

Rain? Thunder?

No, those were footsteps, and not just from a single person.

Cannon dropped his toothbrush and drew his Glock. With his gun pointed down he opened the bathroom door. There were armed men in the hallway. As he raised his gun, someone behind the door kicked it shut, catching his wrist in between the door and the door jamb. The pressure of the door deadened the nerves in his hand, making his fingers release the gun even though he'd been gripping it tightly. He pulled his hand back, but the gun fell to the floor outside.

The door slammed all the way shut and he saw it shudder under the weight of a man's shoulder.

Cannon took inventory of what he'd seen before the door closed. One, two, three, four, five ... six men in the hallway, at least three of them with pistols, and probably all six. All of the guns he'd seen had silencers on them. There was also at least one more man and probably two more behind the door towards Pasha's suite. This was a coordinated and timed attack. Miss Dee would have heard the door slam and tucked Pasha away in her safe corner by now.

If Cannon could take down six of these guys, Miss Dee should be able to handle the other two. Anyone who tried to enter her room without knocking would get a bullet in the chest.

Now Cannon just had to figure out how to stop six guys with only one gun and five bullets. Even if he had more ammo on him, he couldn't start shooting willy-nilly. With such thin walls and doors on this train, hitting innocent passengers was a real possibility.

"Oy," said a man from the other side of the thin bathroom door.

Cannon considered kicking the door open and taking out the man, but he decided to hold off and look for a better plan.

"What do you want?"

"It's not what I want, bodyguard, it's what I'm going to do."

Whatever this guy's plan was, he was confident in it. "I can't hear you," said Cannon. "Crack the door." He turned off the bathroom light, but a night light still partially illuminated the tiny room.

After a few seconds, the door did crack open, giving Cannon the narrow view into the hallway he was looking for. He could see three of the men he knew were there. Out of their view, Cannon pulled his back-up gun, a five-shot revolver, from his ankle holster.

"You don't tell me what to do," grunted the man from behind the door. "Now listen good if you want the little princess to make it off this train alive." The man was about four inches shorter than Cannon, based on where the voice came from. "In ten minutes this train will stop. The princess and the nanny will get off with me, my men, and your cell phone. You and Bruce and Bruce are going to stay behind. They'll keep you company for the next few hours to keep you from making any unauthorized phone calls."

Cannon's blood was boiling and it was all he could do to keep from reaching around the door and breaking this man's neck. No one was going anywhere with Pasha, and no one was going to touch her. Not today, not ever. He was just glad Daisy was far away on another car instead of there with them.

Cannon dug his stun rod out of his pocket with his free hand while he talked. He growled in a voice he knew would carry to every man in the hallway, "I will protect her at any cost, and if you are still out there when I come out, you will pay that cost, not me." Cannon's breathing was fast, and he was in combat mode. "Each and every one of your men better be ready to meet your Maker, because this door will open in ten seconds, and I'm coming out to send you and them to hell."

"That's a tough speech for a man who lost his gun, but this isn't a movie. You're trapped and unarmed and outmanned. Now put your hands out slowly, and everyone can get off this train alive."

"Ten," said Cannon. "Nine." He had no intention of making it to zero. "Eight." At six he would act, while they were still getting ready for him. "Seven."

He heard steps on the staircase. In a split second, conflicting emotions rose: worry for the innocent person about to walk into a deadly standoff, but also gratitude for a minor distraction. But, hold on. He knew that gait.

No no no! Why right now?

This was the Philippines all over again, but instead of Doug running into the line of fire, it was someone he cared about even more, and she didn't even know about the ambush she was running in to. Cannon had to think fast and act decisively.

No, he just had to get her clear.

"Daisy! Run!"

Her steps halted immediately, but through the crack, he saw two men dash to the staircase. A short scuffle ensued, and he heard someone being dragged down the stairs. Daisy was trying to call out, but her voice was muffled.

"Looky here," said the man behind the door, opening the door a few more inches.

Daisy stood there, no longer struggling, with two guns pointed at her head. Cannon controlled his breathing and tried to look at the mission as he would if we were still a SEAL. He had two objectives, two people to protect, but they were in opposite directions and one of them had already been captured.

The man who Cannon still hadn't seen said, "Thanks for coming, *Daisy*. This simplifies things." He tapped on the door with a knuckle. "Oy. Bruce and Bruce are going to take your little lovely back to their room. If you don't cooperate three things are going to happen. You'll die, the princess will still come with us, and there will be no one to make sure Bruce and Bruce behave up there with your lady. Come out now, with your hands up, and you can go with them to make sure things stay civil. It's your decision. How much do you care about these two little ladies?"

Hostage situation. Where was Blayze when he needed him? What would Blayze do in this situation?

He would simplify. He would separate the at-risk parties if possible. Cannon didn't believe for a second that if he gave up, he and Daisy would be safe. Pasha for sure wouldn't be safe. If he did give up and go peacefully, there would be a chance to protect Daisy, but that would mean abandoning Pasha, who had to be his number one priority right now. Would Daisy understand? Had he made his duty clear?

Even if she did understand, could he really do it? Could he really leave Daisy to the fate of the Bruces?

The rules of engagement were clear in his situation, but what about his operational priorities.

Daisy spoke up. "Remember who's number one today."

An ape of a man, who Cannon had to assume was a Bruce, slapped a hand over her mouth. Then he and a short man scooped her up and looked at the man behind the door.

Remember who's number one …

Cannon and Daisy had had that conversation and she said she

wanted to be number one in his book. She *needed* to be first. But that word that she'd thrown on the end there – *today*.

Daisy was talking about Pasha. She wanted him to protect Pasha.

That was good enough for Cannon.

Oh, bless you, Daisy, you brilliant, caring, understanding woman, you.

Now if he could just clear Daisy from this area he could deal with each situation individually.

Cannon told the man on the other side of the door, "This is your last chance. Walk away now or pay the price."

"Get her out of here!" said the man.

Cannon saw Daisy being yanked up the stairs as the bathroom door slammed shut.

Hopefully that helped the situation instead of making it worse. Cannon had never been in such a tight spot, but he wasn't going down without a fight.

WAS CANNON OKAY? Was Pasha? Were any of them going to survive this? Daisy sat crammed into Bruce and Bruce's roomette. This was really happening. Bad guys and guns and she didn't want to think of what else. In a few minutes they'd be at the train station and she had no idea what would happen then. She was scared, more scared than she'd ever been. The two guys had been talking to each other; nasty, filthy things they would do to her if they got the chance. She thought she might vomit at any second.

Right after Bruce and Bruce had dragged her away, she'd heard gunshots! A few really loud ones, and dozens of quiet ones that she assumed came from guns like the ones with silencers that the two Bruces had pointed at her.

"Y-you don't have to keep your fingers on the t-triggers like that," she told them, barely able to speak. She was definitely not James

Bond girlfriend material. She had done enough research in her editing of action scenes to know that a sharp bump of the train or a random loud noise could cause them to accidentally fire the weapons. "Police shoot people all the time by doing that."

They looked at each other, and the little one said, "Can't have her dead if we're going to have some fun with her later."

The thought made Daisy feel dirty, and sick to her stomach again, but at least they put their fingers on the outside of the trigger guard. That comment had been mild compared to some of their other statements. Try as she might, she couldn't unhear their filthy speech.

Little Bruce checked his phone again. Probably waiting for confirmation of what they were supposed to do with her.

Was Cannon okay? Was Pasha? Daisy hoped he'd gotten the message she was trying to send and had somehow tried to protect Pasha instead of some foolish rescue attempt of Daisy. If anything happened to her little sister, Daisy would never forgive herself. Coming on the train again with them hadn't been the best idea. Being around Cannon was good any time, and not having the hope or expectation that he would put her first made it fun even when he was all serious and on duty. But he had a job to do and just by being here, she made that hard for him. She'd never expected anything like this though.

There were a lot of men down there, and a lot of guns, and from what she could see they had Cannon cornered. There was barely room in those bathrooms to turn around, much less try to fight or defend yourself.

And that had been a lot of gunshots. Daisy couldn't think of any way someone could avoid that many gunshots in the small bathroom or even in the narrow hallways of the train.

Tears formed in her eyes and trickled out the edges. She'd never been in love like this before, and now she'd lost him.

Big Bruce's phone chirped from inside his jeans pocket. He

looked at Little Bruce, then started digging it out, which wasn't easy in the tight quarters. She was glad he'd taken his finger off the trigger with all the maneuvering he was attempting.

When he finally retrieved it, his face scrunched up, making him look like a confused monkey. "From the boss," he said to the other Bruce turning the phone.

Daisy was dying to see what the text said.

"Why is he texting you?" Little Bruce ripped the phone away and muttered, "Alive?"

What did that mean? Who was alive? Obviously their boss was or he couldn't be texting them.

Daisy considered lashing out while they were distracted. Would well-placed kicks to the groin give her enough time to run? Or could she grab a gun away? And if she did, could she really shoot someone?

Yes, in the case of these two pieces of filth, she thought she could. Actually getting a gun away was the part of the plan she doubted she could do.

Big Bruce said, "He must want me to be in charge now. So, let's, uh, we should ..." He scratched his temple with the tip of his silencer. "What should we do?"

Little Bruce leaned forward. They both smelled like cigarette smoke and old sweat. "Get her back to the alpha car," said Little Bruce. He waved his gun at Daisy. "Up, hot stuff."

"Is ... is Cannon alive?" she asked, not budging.

Little Bruce sneered. "No. So sorry, but your boyfriend decided to play the hero."

"I'm not going anywhere," said Daisy with a tremble in her bottom lip.

"We can make you," he said, raising the gun to her face.

"Bu-ut, your boss wants me alive." Maybe that's what the text had said. It was worth a shot.

Uncertainty flashed across his face, but he covered it quickly. "No, he said that if you come nicely, the princess will stay alive."

"That's a lie." If Cannon really was ... dead, then Daisy was in even more trouble than before. She had to try to be smart about this, and brave.

"If you don't want to come nicely, I can shoot both of your feet and give Bruce a reason to carry you." His sneering smile turned cruel. "Or if you don't want to come, I can gag you and just leave you alone in here with big, cuddly Bruce for a while."

Big Bruce's eyes went wide and he licked his lips.

Tears were welling in her eyes and bile was rising in her throat. "Fine, I'll go. "

"Don't try anything," said Little Bruce. "Because now, my finger is on the trigger."

PLEASE, *Lord, let me be a weapon in your hand, so I can protect those in my care against men with evil intent,* said Cannon in a silent prayer.

Daisy was gone. Safely out of the fighting zone for the moment. It was time for action.

The man on the other side of the bathroom door yelled, "You just made a big mis—"

Cannon put a bullet through the door where the man's face was and followed with two in the chest, shutting him up immediately. The three shots reverberated through the bathroom like, well, cannon shots. He jumped up onto the counter, with one foot in the sink, smashed the nightlight, and conformed his body to the mirror and ceiling. As he had expected, bullets like a hailstorm poured through the thin door and out the wall of the train. They were all suppressed, sounding like popcorn going off on hot grease. If he had been standing on the floor, he'd have taken twenty wounds or more.

The barrage lasted a few seconds, and Cannon felt a sharp jolt pass through his calf, but he didn't feel any pain. Not yet anyway. When the shooting stopped, Cannon stayed put. He had an idea of how these men would operate and he knew they couldn't go for Pasha until they were confident Cannon was out of the way.

Seconds passed like hours, but this was not Cannon's first fire fight and he waited ... waited ... waited. Shadows shifted in the hallway, changing the faint light patterns that came through the door.

Wait for it, he calmly told himself.

A second onslaught of bullets came, not as heavy as the first, but just as deadly if he'd been standing in the wrong spot. With this volley, they had shot high and low. Not quite high enough to hit him, but the door was Swiss cheese.

When that stream of bullets ended, Cannon heard someone whisper, "Check it."

The outline of a face appeared and Cannon shot without hesitation and without remorse. These men were as bad as the cowardly men in Iraq who tortured and killed women and children.

Immediately after shooting, Cannon dropped to the floor and barreled through the door. He collided with one man, sending him off balance. Cannon whipped the stun rod out and jabbed it in the direction of Pasha's door without even looking. Sure enough, it made impact with someone who took the jolt of the stun rod full in the chest.

As bullets started flying down the hall from the other direction, Cannon grabbed the man he'd collided with and turned him to use him as a shield. His companions filled the man with bullets, some of which passed through and struck Cannon. The shield's legs went out and Cannon dropped to his knees behind the corpse.

"Now, Miss Dee!" With his last bullet, Cannon took out the nearest guy from a kneeling position.

Behind him, he heard the door to the suite fly open and two quick shots boomed out as Miss Dee shot over Cannon's head, knocking the last man off his feet. They'd arranged in the past that if it ever came to a shootout, Cannon would shoot low, since he'd most likely be in the line of fire, and Miss Dee would shoot high.

"Cover him," ordered Cannon, pointing to the one he'd dropped with the stun rod. She dropped to one knee to reduce her profile, and Cannon rushed forward, needing to be sure all of the men were down. He covered the thirty feet of hallway in no time, and confirmed that there were no more shooters.

On the way back, he checked each man to make sure that they were really down, and not playing possum.

"Pasha?" asked Cannon when he reached Miss Dee.

"She's fine."

"Are you okay?"

"I am," said Miss Dee. "But you're shot."

"I know." Looking down at his calf made the pain finally register.

"Here too," said Miss Dee, pointing at his right shoulder and the left side of his abdomen. "I'll have paramedics meet us at the train station in Sacramento. Police also."

"There are two more men," said Cannon. "I have to get to them before we stop in Sacramento." Leaving Pasha felt like leaving a man behind in combat, but he'd done what he could here. If Bruce and Bruce didn't see their companions get off the train in Sacramento, they would most likely kill Daisy and exit the train quietly, expecting her to not be discovered until Seattle.

Miss Dee didn't look convinced. He considered making up an excuse about not being able to rest until all of their attackers were dealt with, but it came down to needing to rescue Daisy.

"I'm going," he told her, then turned to the guy on the ground. "Where are they? Where did Bruce and Bruce take her?"

The guy was wide-eyed, laying on his side, hands up in surrender.

"I don't have a lot of time," said Cannon. "But I have a lot of ideas how to make you talk."

The man glanced up the hallway at the bodies. "Room six on the next car."

Cannon popped into his room and grabbed a set of handcuffs from his bag. As he slapped them on the prisoner, he said, "If you're lying, I'll make you sorry." There was only one good shot at a rescue; Cannon needed good intel.

"I'm not lying. I swear."

Cannon looked at Miss Dee. "I'll send Felix down to watch this guy. When you see Felix, close the door and don't open it for anyone but me."

Miss Dee's mouth was pinched. "Mr. Gold will not be pleased if you leave."

There was no question what Cannon had to do, and he didn't care right now about Mr. Gold. He grabbed a few more gadgets from his room.

"Keep her safe," said Cannon, turning to the stairwell. He climbed cautiously, watching for any more surprises. At the top of stairs, he found a cautious Felix, standing by, but staying clear. "Pasha and Miss Dee are fine, but there are some dead men down there. I need you to keep an eye on one man in handcuffs in the aisle and also alert Miss Dee if anyone else approaches. But first, call Gustav. Have him meet me right here."

THE BARREL of the gun in Daisy's back felt like a dagger that was about to puncture her spine. Daisy was so terrified she could barely stand.

Before heading back to the alpha car, as one of the Bruce's had called it, the three of them got carefully arranged with Big Bruce in the front, then Daisy, followed by Little Bruce with his gun digging into her back.

That trigger finger made her nervous. Her armpits were working overtime, sweating with every bounce, jerk, and rumble of the train. One of Camille Jackson's novels dealt with a concept called bimanual synkinesis. It's what she had mentioned to the Bruces in their roomette. When one hand makes a movement, the other hand often mirrors it subconsciously.

Never did she think she'd use that obscure knowledge, and never with her on the barrel end of a gun.

The storm raged outside, thunder and rain. Still, after the commotion in the front car, she expected people sticking their heads out, concealed carry people coming out of the woodwork, and maybe an overhead announcement to duck and cover. The thunder and the mechanical noises and late hour explained the lack of alarm in this car, but people in the front car had to have heard the gunshots, at least the ones that weren't suppressed. And even if they mistook those for sounds from the engine, it would still alarm people, right?

Daisy considered calling out for help, or trying to squirm away from Little Bruce and duck into a bedroom. But not only did she not know which ones were locked and which were unlocked, she would probably just be endangering an innocent stranger if she did that.

Someone was down at the end of the car by the stairs, but she couldn't make out who it was. Little Bruce had told Big Bruce to move at a slow pace, to make it easier to stick together. As she got closer, Daisy saw that it was Gustav, the dining car host! Maybe she could make eye contact with him and alert him that something was wrong without causing a huge scene. They had to have hostage protocols in the train system, right?

As they approached, Daisy stared daggers and called out mentally to Gustav, but he was super intent on whatever he was doing with the coffee machine. He didn't even notice them coming. The most they would get out of him would be a grunt and a nod.

Her one chance of rescue was about to pass.

When Big Bruce was about three steps from Gustav, Daisy

noticed a door next to her that was open. The curtains were drawn, and just as she stepped past they parted, and a hand holding something metal came down right behind her back. It hit Little Bruce's arm with a crack and she heard his gun clatter to the floor.

Daisy screamed in reflex. The jolt made her jump and she still kind of wondered if she'd been shot and just hadn't felt it yet.

Cannon stepped out of the roomette and grabbed Little Bruce around the neck. Daisy had to pinch herself twice to make sure she hadn't gone off in some rescue fantasy, but this was really happening! Cannon bent and twisted himself, then Little Bruce rose up off the ground a foot, only to come down with accelerated force, face-first into Cannon's shoulder. Little Bruce fell to the floor unconscious.

Daisy swiveled her head and saw Big Bruce starting to turn toward her. Gustav shot him in the side of the face with a Taser and for good measure jabbed another stun device into his neck. The big guy shook like Jell-O in an earthquake.

Cannon darted past Daisy and guided Big Bruce to the ground, face down with his arms behind his back. In about one second, he had Big Bruce in handcuffs.

Daisy was glued in place, thinking that maybe everything was fine now, but still not comprehending how it had happened.

Cannon stood from slapping another set of cuffs on Little Bruce then took both of Daisy's arms in his.

Automatically, she muttered, "Snicker-snack."

Cannon's eyebrows went up, searching her face as if she'd gone mad. "Did they hurt you, Daisy?"

She searched for the words, still unsure. "Um, no." The world was starting to make sense. He had done it. He had rescued her. Bruce and Bruce were in handcuffs on the ground and they couldn't do anything to her now. Daisy burrowed in his chest and wrapped her arms tight around him, still trembling like a leaf in the wind.

He put his arms around her, but she could feel his neck swiveling, still keeping an eye on the scene.

"What was that?" she asked. "Who ...?"

"They wanted to kidnap Pasha," said Cannon. "The police or FBI will have to investigate."

"Pasha! Is she okay?" Her expression grew frantic as she looked toward Pasha's car.

"She's fine." He placed his palm on her cheek and she leaned into it.

"You saved me," she said, gratitude and love for him causing her eyes to fill with tears again.

"Daisy, I'm so sorry I let them take you."

"You did the right thing," she sniffled.

He didn't seem to hear her and kept explaining. "I know you want to be first in my book and under any other circumstances, I would—" He paused and looked at her with a perplexed expression on his face. "What did you say?"

She had to lean back a bit to look up into his face, but still craved the safety of his arms and wanted them tighter around her again. "I'm glad you stayed to protect Pasha."

"You are?"

Daisy nodded, smiling at his puzzlement. Then with a sigh she said, "I'm sorry it was such a hard decision for you."

"So you did mean for me to stay? That's what your code was?"

"One hundred percent. I don't want a guy who doesn't believe in duty or loyalty. Or one who would put my safety in front of that of a child."

He pulled her back in tight and just squeezed her for a second.

She asked, "How'd you know we'd be coming right now and they wouldn't shoot me?"

He pulled a cell phone out of his pants pocket. "I told them I needed you alive at any cost. And I knew if I could catch him on the wrist, he'd drop the gun. It's what happened to me with the bath-room door."

Cannon held her out a bit so they could see each other's faces. "You are the most important thing to me, Daisy. Two days a week I work, that's all."

"And I get you the other five days of the week?" she asked.

"You get all of me," he said eagerly. "I realized during all this ... I love you, Daisy. More than I can say."

"I love you too," she said, goose bumps rising up and down her arms.

They smiled at each other and she knew that this man who had put his life on the line for her, for Pasha, for anyone who was defenseless, was the best man alive. He didn't just throw around words like honor and duty and love of God—he lived it. And she, Daisy Mae Close, was the one he loved, the one he wanted to be with. It was more perfect than any fantasy she could come up with.

Cannon said, "We need to get back to the front car, but first ..." he leaned in and kissed her. Daisy kissed back hungrily. This man had come for her, had risked his life to rescue her. The power and passion of the kiss told her that he'd been every bit as scared as she had been. When he deepened the kiss, she rose to meet him, giving every bit as much as taking.

The kiss was too short, but she knew they had to go. And she planned on many more encounters like that, on her time, with her real boyfriend, when she was all his.

As she lowered from him, she noticed her hand was wet, and when she looked closer, she saw it was blood.

"You're hurt!"

"Just a little gun shot. Nothing life-threatening."

"Little gun shot!" What was he talking about? "Where?"

"Shoulder and calf. Oh, and a graze on my bicep. And one on my side."

"What? You need to lie down! Should I tie a tourniquet? Why are you acting like this is no big deal?"

Cannon chuckled. "One question at a time, and wait until we get back to the other car. I went through worse than this on a daily basis in BUD/S training."

Daisy couldn't believe it. Maybe he was messing with her. If he'd really been shot he wouldn't be playing it off like this, would he?

He took her by the hand and turned toward Gustav.

"I can't thank you enough," said Cannon.

"I live to serve," said Gustav with a little bow. "It was worth it to get to play with your toys."

"Will you make that announcement and keep an eye on these two?" asked Cannon.

"Right away, boss."

As Cannon and Daisy made their way toward the lead car— Cannon limping because he'd been shot!— she heard Gustav's announcement.

Ladies and gentlemen, I apologize for disturbing you, but we will have an extended stop in Sacramento. If there are any law enforcement passengers, or doctors or paramedics, please come to the front car if you are willing to assist us.

Well, that would freak people out. But given the choice between knowing what kind of violence had transpired versus being in the dark, the people with limited knowledge were better off.

Either way, Daisy had nothing to worry about. Her real boyfriend had made the right choice and protected Pasha. He had somehow survived about a million gunshots, even though he didn't seem to notice the ones that had hit him—what did she expect from a former SEAL?—and she was safe and back with him.

Once again, Daisy gave herself a pinch but nothing changed. Somehow her real life had become even more wonderful than her fantasy life.

12

Saturday night, eight days after the train incident, Cannon pulled up to Daisy's house and climbed out of his SUV. After two days in England, he couldn't wait to see her.

She didn't even let him make it to the door but busted through it as he was walking up the steps and leaped into his arms. Her blonde hair covered his face, and he breathed in deeply her clean, yummy smell.

"I missed you," he said, leaning back to see her beautiful, carefree face. Being with his buddies, pulling off an incredible mission, and performing a wedding on foreign soil had been extremely satisfying, but nothing compared with this woman who embodied everything good in the world, everything that made life worth living for him.

"You smell like an airplane," said Daisy playfully.

"See if I taste like one." He kissed her, even as she laughed, but she quickly returned the kiss. Oh, it was good to be back in the U.S. of A. It might have been his imagination, but Daisy always seemed to be smiling when he kissed her? Was it the natural shape of her lips, or was it just how he felt when he was around her, like all of the darkness he'd experienced was inert. The world was a bright place. Everything was going to be great.

"Mm," she said, licking her lips. "Definitely not airplane. Thanks for coming straight here. How are your massive injuries?"

"My mere flesh wounds? Healing nicely. I barely notice them."

It was obvious by her expression that she didn't believe him. "And your jetlag?"

"Nothing compared with being awake on the train for 36 hours every week."

"Come inside," she said, pulling him up the walk. "Did you find out anything about the train stuff?"

"The FBI is investigating still. They think it was an attempt to get a huge ransom." The rest of the topic would pull some of the joy out of his world, but luckily Daisy was here to keep him from feeling it. "I talked to Rasmus in the car on the way here."

She must have sensed his disappointment because she turned to him with a frown once they were inside. "There's more?"

"Rasmus and his ex have decided that as much as Pasha loves train trips, it's not a reasonable mode of travel for her any longer. Sutton and I advised them of the same right after the incident, so it's partially our fault."

He was going to miss those long trips with that other little bright spot in his life. Why was he getting emotional about it? He'd still see her.

Cannon grunted away the ball in his throat and said, "She'll be flying on daddy's private jet back and forth between California and Washington from now on."

"Oh, Cannon, I'm sorry." She put a hand on his injured shoulder and he didn't flinch. By not reacting when she touched his wounds, it kept her guessing, trying to remember which arm and which leg had been injured.

"He still wants me to provide security." Miss Dee had been

wrong about Rasmus not being happy. He was bowled over with emotion when he heard about the overwhelming odds against his little girl, said Cannon was obviously a superhero of some sort, and had told everyone involved that Cannon had handled the situation exactly right.

"That's wonderful!" said Daisy.

"Yeah. He was extremely grateful that everything turned out so well for the good guys on the train."

Daisy looked at her hand on his shoulder and slowly lifted it as she looked up to study his face. For a while they just looked at each other, and again Cannon knew she was all he needed in the world.

"This is the hurt shoulder, isn't it? Why do you have to stand there and suffer in silence?" She bent and pulled back his sport coat and kissed his shoulder, making electricity shoot up his spine. "Why don't you ever tell me?"

Cannon chuckled. "And risk having you touch me less? No way."

She gave him a seductive look, with a little rise of her eyebrows and said, "Maybe I'd touch you more."

Cannon's mouth went dry and he felt himself blush hard.

That made her smile. "Come over here and talk to me while I finish getting ready." She went into the bathroom and started putting some makeup on. "Same work schedule? Friday and Saturday?"

Cannon leaned against the wall in the hallway. "No, just Friday morning." He wasn't sure he wanted to tell her the next part. It was hard to explain his reasoning to someone who didn't understand right from the start. He decided to give it a try. "Rasmus wanted to give me a big reward for ... for doing my job. I say big reward, and for me it is big, but for him it's chump change. A quarter mill."

Daisy's eyebrows went up in disbelief and her makeup stick froze halfway to her face.

Cannon went on. "I turned him down. But he was super insistent."

"That's really nice of him," said Daisy, putting half of her attention back on the mirror. She picked up some kind of pinching iron thing and started flattening her hair.

"He gave Gustav and Felix a reward also. He said something about matching their annual salary."

"Wow. That says a lot about how much he cares about his daughter." She sprayed something in her hair and then ironed it again. "Especially since she's not even riding the train any longer."

"I'm not taking the money," said Cannon. She was going to think he was crazy. She might even try to convince him to change his mind. "The thought of it makes me feel like a sell-out."

"That is so ..." She put the hair implement down and walked over to him and locked eyes with him again. "So ... like you."

Already on the defensive, he wasn't sure how to take that, since everyone else he knew would be making fun of him for it.

She was smiling up at him. "How lucky am I to have the only real boyfriend in the world who would turn down that much money strictly on principle?" She kissed him tenderly, then went back to her hair routine.

Well, that answered that. How lucky was he to have someone who would let that much money go without trying to convince him to reconsider? "Rasmus kept insisting, so I came up with an idea."

Daisy raised an eyebrow, her interest piqued again.

"I'm going to start a ministry." He hadn't told anyone yet, and saying it out loud made him start sweating. "He's going to donate the two hundred and fifty grand as soon as I get it set up." The nagging doubt struck up again and he looked down at the floor. Who was he —a soldier, a killer—to claim to be a worthy servant of the Lord? Yeah, he'd counseled other soldiers, greeted churchgoers at the door, led the occasional Bible study, helped the youth in the church with some fundraisers, and done some custodial work, but all those things could be done despite the blood on his hands. This was a whole new level of taking authority he wasn't sure he deserved.

Daisy appeared in his view, peeking up into his posture. "Hey, where's that patented Cannon Culver, life-is-good smile? You should be thrilled about this. You're going to do so much good."

Oh that was right. Now he remembered. He was someone who tried to amplify the light in the world. He was a man who would fight darkness with his last breath. He was best friends with the brightest five-year-old girl in the world. And he was boyfriend to the perfect woman.

"There it is," she said, putting a hand on his cheek. "What's wrong?"

Cannon could sense the doubts on the edges of his perception still, and he got all teary-eyed. He could tell her, right? She wouldn't think he was crazy or stupid or presumptuous, right? "I just keep wondering what makes me think I'm worthy? After all I've been through, after all I've done. A bunch of Bible verses keep running through my head. *No man takes this honor on himself. I am not fit to untie the thong of his sandals. Depart from me Lord, for I am a sinful—*"

"Hey," said Daisy, putting a finger to his quivering lips. A tear broke from one eye and ran all the way down his face. She wiped it and asked, "Did Jesus turn any of them away?"

"What?"

"The people who said those things. Did he ever tell them they were unworthy, or were those just their own doubts?"

Cannon thought. As far as he knew, Jesus never told any sincere person anything like that. Wow, why had he never considered that before?

Daisy nodded, seeing the realization on his face. "You are worthy. He needs someone like you. The world needs someone like you. Now, what's the focus of the ministry going to be?"

With his confidence renewed, the answer came easily. "There's a lot of bad in the world and there's a lot of kids who grow up surrounded by it. But there's a lot of good too. I want to help inner city kids see the good, and focus on it. Whether that's through sports, or the outdoors, or computer programming, or service. Whatever, I just want to bring in mentors to help them see that the good is there, if they just go find it."

Daisy was still watching him with those supportive eyes of hers so he went on. "I'm almost positive I can team up with the church, so if the kids want to learn about Jesus, they'll have the opportunity, but it won't be required."

"I ... couldn't be prouder," said Daisy. "You're the best man I know."

That made Cannon even more emotional and he had to deflect or he'd start bawling again. "And you're going to be late for your big night if you don't finish getting ready."

She went back to the bathroom counter and looked herself over, then picked up a lipstick.

"Wait," he said, catching her in a funny, pursed-lips face. He kissed those lips, sliding his hand carefully behind her neck and she was quick to respond. In the three-day turnaround for his trip to England, he'd missed her more than he expected. Not just her lips, but how he felt around her.

As much as he wanted to just keep kissing her, they did have somewhere to be.

"Good idea getting that done before I got this on." She went back to her makeup.

"Oh, there's still no guarantee I won't mess it up later."

"That sounds fun." She smiled at him as she walked past him and into her bedroom. "And I really think dusky rose is your color, which is good because I'm pretty sure you'll be wearing some of it by the end of the night."

He laughed and walked into the front room as she closed her door. Being here with her, and just having her in his life made him feel like the Lord knew him and wanted to tell Cannon that he was on the right path. Bad things would still come up in his life, but with a companion like Daisy, he could face them without letting them define him. And for the first time in his life, he thought he might actually feel worthy.

She came out a couple minutes later, backing out of the room. "Zip me up?"

Cannon couldn't resist admiring her smooth skin just begging to be touched, and he ran a finger up her spine as he reached for the zipper.

"Mmm," she moaned, doing a little shiver. "Those are the best goose bumps I've ever had."

He smile and pinched the zipper, carefully tugging it upward. It felt fragile enough to rip off without even trying.

When he was done, she let her hair fall into place, then spun and held her arms out, showing off the little black dress she was wearing "How do I look?"

"You look better than a pizza and nap at the end of BUD/S."

It was her turn to laugh and she came over to hug him and rest her head on his chest. He was careful not to mess up her hair or makeup.

"You look gorgeous," he told her. "But I have to admit that you are always this beautiful to me. It's your inner beauty, and how you help me see the good things in the world." He kissed her gently on the forehead. "Come on. I can't wait to see you win your big award tonight."

She let him go and handed him her fancy jacket, which he helped her put on. "There is some dang stiff competition, and freelance editors never really win awards like this, so don't be disappointed if I don't pull a Cannon and achieve some superhuman feat in the face of impossible odds."

"Oh great," he said, "now I have to deal with unattainable expectations for the next fifty years."

"Only I know your real secret," she said, leading him to the door and locking it behind them. "You're a wizard, like Harry Dresden. You are unstoppable."

Grateful to escape the praise, he opened the car door for her and she climbed in.

They drove to his place, where he did a quick shower, shave, and change, then came out in a tuxedo. Of course it had some custom pockets for his gadgets. Not that anything would happen tonight at the fancy North American Book Awards banquet.

When she saw him, she wolf-whistled and said, "My daydream about this moment wasn't nearly as good as the real thing." She put a hand on his freshly-shaven cheek and rubbed it for a minute. If the event wasn't such a big deal he would've tried to get her to just stay in.

Cannon said, "If I look half as good as you do, we're a shoe-in for hottest couple tonight."

"Thanks, but I checked out the website and that isn't an actual award there."

"Oh well. Guess we'll settle for Best Editor—Multiple Works." He looked down at her lips and asked, "Is that lipstick dry yet? We should probably practice for the celebratory kiss."

"Lipstick doesn't dry," she said, rolling her eyes. "It's like you've never had a real girlfriend or something."

"Why do you say that?" he asked. "*Real* boyfriend and *real* girlfriend?"

A guilty look crossed her face. He'd seen it enough to be sure that's what it was and he could feel his own smile twisting in response.

"You're busted," he told her. "So tell me."

"I know I'm busted," she sighed. "I can tell by your little amused smile. At least let's get in the car so I can think of how to describe it without embarrassing myself."

He helped her into the car and as they pulled into the frustrating Saturday night L.A. traffic, she explained, "I do this thing in my head where I make up stories in my life. I think it's a side effect of my job but I always paint it as more exciting and glamorous than it really is.

Actually, I should say I *used to* do that. Since I started palling around with you, real life is more exciting than fantasy."

"Wait!" he interjected excitedly. "You used to like zone out, like you were having a minor seizure or something. Mind switching. Was that the same thing?"

Her face turned red, and she refused to look at him. "Yes."

He couldn't help cracking up. "Oh, I love that so much. Ha ha ha. I was just asking if you minded switching seats, but I could tell by your face that you thought you'd been busted. Oh, man, that is hilarious."

"If you're done over there ..." She waited until he had his smile under control. "In addition to making up fantasy events, I also used to think of cute guys as my fake boyfriend."

Cannon felt his eyebrows shoot up, but he bit his tongue because he was dying to find out more and didn't want to interrupt her.

"And I know you're going to ask, so I'll just tell you. Yes, you were my fake boyfriend way before you were my real boyfriend. That's why I say real boyfriend now because it's literally a dream come true."

"When—"

"I knew you were going to ask that too." She looked over at him, and he could feel her studying his face. "You weren't even all the way in the train car yet and I had already claimed you as my fake boyfriend." She hesitated and he could tell she was on the fence about admitting something else.

"Go ahead and say it," he said.

"Ugh. I need to figure out how to keep secrets from you. Okay, fine. When you first walked in, I thought you were a little family. I thought Miss Dee and you were ... Pasha's parents."

Cannon lost it for a second, laughing so hard he could barely keep his eyes on the road. Never in a million years could he be with someone as formal as Miss Dee. "She's great at her job, the best, and

I'm glad Pasha has her, but it would be torture for me to be in a relationship with someone all stiff and pragmatic like her."

"I'm so glad you're enjoying this," she told him, but she had to admit it was funny to look back on. "So of course if you were married, you couldn't be my fake boyfriend, but as soon as I learned you weren't Pasha's parents, you were my on-again fake boyfriend."

"And to think, you made me so nervous I could barely talk."

"Yeah right," she said, rolling her eyes.

"Wanna know something? I play, well *played*, a little game on the trains. When I heard footsteps on the stairs, I'd paint a picture in my mind. Like, old overweight guy with a mustache. Twin teenage boys in Polo shirts. A woman in jeans with a buzz cut and nose ring. I could usually get the big picture right, but the only time I nailed every detail was when I guessed beautiful woman in her mid 20's. Blonde hair, blue eyes, one dimple and a smile that can light up a room."

Her face lit up. "You identified me from my steps on the stairs."

"I wish I could take credit," he said. "I think it was more of wishful thinking and serendipity."

She leaned over and squeezed his uninjured shoulder. "I loved that night. I know we won't be on the train any more, but I want more of those late nights with you."

"I can't wait," he said.

They pulled into the event center parking lot, and Daisy handed over a pass that he gave to the attendant. They parked and walked arm in arm toward the banquet area. Even though it was fun to dress up, drive the fancy company car, and eat an expensive dinner, Cannon only really cared about being with Daisy. The rest was great, and he would enjoy every minute of it, but he didn't need it.

Before they went in the door, Cannon turned to face her. "I am all yours tonight," he told her. "I don't care if aliens land and offer free spaceship rides, I'm not leaving your side."

"What are you talking about?" she said. "We'd go see the Milky Way together."

"As long as I'm with you," he told her. "Oh, and here, you better have this for good luck." He bent and kissed her slowly, savoring the softness of her lips.

"Mm," she said a moment later. "I feel like I already got lucky."

He pulled the door open and said, "After you, Best Editor— Multiple Works nominee."

They stopped at the coat check and Daisy handed over her jacket.

"Hold on," said Cannon, pulling his phone out and sliding it into Daisy's pocket.

As if on cue, it started buzzing. Cannon shrugged and turned away from it. He didn't get many phone calls, so he wondered who it was, but it could wait a few hours.

Her smile was reward enough, and sliding her arm into the crook of his was a bonus.

Three hundred places or more were set in the banquet hall. When Cannon and Daisy entered, an usher led them to the front of the room to one of the tables closest to the stage. Another couple was already seated, people who Daisy didn't recognize. After introductions, they made small talk. The couple were both retired doctors and patrons of the North American Literature Society. They had a million questions for Daisy once they learned she was a nominee.

Cannon's Coms band buzzed. On the outside it looked like a normal silver band. When it was activated, blue LED lights ran along it. On the inside he could receive messages. Casually, he slipped it off his wrist.

Come in. Urgent.

Sutton hardly ever used the Coms band. Did this have something to do with the attempted kidnapping? Was someone in danger? Were he and Daisy in danger?

"What is it?" she said, worry pulling the corners of her eyes down.

"It's ... it'll have to wait." He knew she could read the worry on his own face, but tried to brush it off.

"Are you sure?" she asked quietly. "I know you deal with life and death situations, and even though it's hard, I understand."

Cannon slid the Coms band into his suit coat pocket. "It can wait."

She squeezed his hand and they turned back to the conversation. In rapid succession, the other two couples arrived to fill the table. Cannon did his best to relax and be social, but his index of suspicion was raised so he was also keeping an eye on the room as a whole to gauge potential threats.

With the rest of the table filled, he and Daisy were able to sit back a bit more and enjoy each other's company and the growing excitement for the awards ceremony. Cannon ignored the repeated vibrating of the Coms device in his pocket.

A suspicious-looking usher entered the room, scanning and moving between the tables. When he locked eyes with Cannon, he made a beeline for him. As the man neared their table, Cannon turned himself to interpose between the man and Daisy and did a mental inventory of all the non-lethal gadgets he carried. Cannon also had to watch behind himself and to the sides to make sure this guy wasn't just a diversion.

"Mr. Culver," said the usher, coming to a stop and performing a little bow.

"Yes?"

"There is an urgent call for you in the lobby."

Why now? Why tonight? "It's going to have to wait."

"Cannon," said Daisy softly.

Leaning closer the usher said, "It appears to be a matter of life and death. The caller identified himself as the Warrior's Heart."

That was his team for sure. Something was seriously wrong.

Cannon kept wondering if the threat was for him and Daisy, but he had no supporting evidence and his gut said they were safe, even though they definitely had some enemies after last week on the train. Was Pasha okay? Maybe Sutton needed to convey information regarding her.

"You have to take it," said Daisy. "We still have an hour until the awards start."

In a whisper he replied, "I'm only taking it so I can make sure we are safe."

"Can I ... can I go with you?"

That made Cannon's heart soar despite his worry. "I wouldn't have it any other way." Tonight he had only one objective, so he wanted to keep her close.

To the table, Daisy said, "Excuse us, please."

As they followed the usher out of the room, Cannon checked their backs and just kept repeating to himself, *Why, why, why did it have to be tonight?*

DAISY FOLLOWED the usher out of the banquet hall, keeping one hand in Cannon's and feeling safe with him at her back. It almost felt like the dance he used to do on the train, keeping Pasha covered at all times.

Something was very wrong. This was not just a matter of one of Cannon's buddies just wanting to reach out and say hi. The look on his face as he'd scanned that spy bracelet of his made her expect bullets to start flying at any moment. With Cannon, you could never be sure that wouldn't happen.

Daisy was back to her old conflict. She wanted to support him, and she knew this was important, but once again, he was going to rush off to deal with something more important than her, and on this night of all nights that she'd been looking forward to.

At the coat check area, the attendant handed him a phone.

"Who is this?" demanded Cannon.

Daisy wasn't close enough to hear everything but she did catch a man's voice, a military voice.

Cannon said, "Culver. Bravo three six."

In the car after the fight on the beach he'd given a similar code but different letter and numbers.

From the phone, she heard bits and pieces. "... bad, completely destroyed ... word from Sutton ... don't know if Liz ... "

"And Agatha?" asked Cannon.

A garbled response was all the reply Daisy heard, but Cannon's face fell, then his jaw clenched and she recognized the protector Cannon coming out. Someone had hurt someone he loved, and more than likely would pay for it.

The man on the phone said another string of words, but all Daisy caught was "boys ... ever since ... incommunicado."

Cannon stared blankly into the coats and the phone fell away from his ear an inch or two.

"Big Gun," said the voice, "you still with me?"

"Tell me one more time. Sutton's exact words."

Cannon was still giving the earpiece some space. The voice said, "Tell the Warriors I said, 'Come in, boys.'"

Again Cannon went somewhere else. This must be what it looked like back when Daisy used to go away into her fantasy worlds. Just as quickly, he snapped back to reality and said, "I can't make it, Zane. I'll check back in six hours."

"Culver," demanded the voice. "We need everyone. Yesterday."

"No can do. Not for another six hours."

"This is not a request. It's a mandatory—"

"With due respect, Zane. You're not my CO any more. I'll see you in six hours." Cannon handed the phone back to the attendant, thanked him, and turned away. He held an arm out for Daisy as if he was ready to just escort her back to her table.

She accepted it only long enough to pull him away from listening ears to a quiet corner of the lobby. "That sounded important. Are your guys okay?"

"I'm ... not really sure."

Daisy took a deep breath and considered for half a second, but it was clear what she had to do. They would probably call it taking one for the team. "You need to go, Cannon." How did this keep happening? Was she destined to lose him over and over and over? He wasn't even a soldier any more. But she loved him, and this was probably one of those times where she needed to give instead of take.

He shook his head. "The only place I'm going is back in there to watch you win your award."

Daisy felt petty for making such a big deal about something so inconsequential in the scheme of things. "I'm pretty sure you have a duty," she told him. "You owe it to those boys."

"The boys," said Cannon, shaking his head with a sardonic chuckle. More to himself than to her, he said, "Leave it to Sutton to send such a subtle clue in his biggest hour of need. He's *never* called us boys in his life."

"What is it?" asked Daisy. "What happened?"

Cannon grew serious, looking down at her with those mesmerizing emerald eyes. "What happened is I've decided it's time to put off childish things. The boys come second from now on. You are my Team now."

Her view of his face glistened behind happy tears to hear him say that and she savored the sentiment for a minute before saying, "But they have a real emergency. People are hurt, I don't know, maybe even ... dead." That word had never bothered her before when it was just something used in fiction, but now it had become a reality and she hated saying it. "This banquet, this event is just ..." She didn't even know how to compare it.

With no hesitation, he said, "It's important. Any other night, I would rush out. But I made a promise to you tonight."

"What about your promises to your guys?"

"I've already left you too many times," he insisted. "Putting other people's needs in front of the needs of the woman I love is just as bad as putting my needs before yours."

Daisy loved hearing those words, *the woman I love*, and they almost convinced her to give in. "But there's nothing you can do here. Either I won or I didn't, and you being in the audience isn't going to change that."

"Me hollering like a crazed football fan when you take the stage will make a difference. It'll be a night the literary boosters never forget."

Daisy had to grin at that. "Please promise me you won't do that. I still have to work with a lot of these people."

"Can I yell, 'Snicker-snack!'?"

Daisy chuckled, wondering if he really would.

"You ready to go back in?" he asked.

"I'm not convinced," she said. "I don't want you to resent me for keeping you away when they might be ... when they might really need you."

"If they are that bad off, then there really is nothing I can do by the time I meet up with them. Daisy," his gaze grew even more intense as if he'd sharpened the focus on her. "If I don't have you in my life ..." his mouth closed and his lips drew tight together in a line, like he was trying to keep in overwhelming emotion and barely succeeding. He tried again. "If I don't have you in my life, then what is the point of having anything else?"

Daisy had thought she was smitten before, but every minute together she was more in love with this man.

He broke eye contact for a second, looking up at the ceiling, pondering. "How do I explain how important this is to me? If I can't prove to you here and now, tonight, that you are the most important thing in my life, then I will never be able to prove it."

He kissed her, leaving her even more stunned.

"I love you," he said, and kissed her again.

"I need you," another kiss. It was getting harder and harder to let him pull away with each kiss. And her argument to get him to go was crumbling.

Cupping her face in both hands, he finished by saying, "And I will prove to you that I have put away childish things, and I am ready to be a man, as long as you are my woman."

"Oh, Cannon." What else could she say? She threw herself into his arms, forcing him to catch her, and pulled him tight for another kiss, good and long. She couldn't believe this man had turned such a one-eighty from where he was with her on their first date. "Are you sure there's nothing I can do to convince you to go?"

"Not in a million years."

"Well then, we have a party to get to." She reached up and wiped the lipstick off his mouth. Most of it anyway. She didn't care if anyone suspected she'd been out here kissing her super handsome bona fide boyfriend.

Cannon held out his arm and they walked back into the banquet hall with her feeling like the most important person in the world.

EPILOGUE

It was my wedding day. I was standing in the highest room of the castle, looking out over the kingdom that would be mine today after I married the Prince. But his castle and his gold and his position meant nothing. Today the bravest, strongest, most handsome and caring man in the world would be mine and I would be his for the rest of our lives.

Daisy grinned to herself and looked out from an upstairs window in Sutton Smith's mansion. The views of San Diego Bay were breathtaking, but she was more focused on the gathering below on his massive back lawn. Everyone in the world she loved was there, and standing at the front looking better than ever was the man she loved. The man who she could spend her life with after today.

"Get away from that window!" said Talia. "You know you aren't supposed to see the groom before the wedding."

"I think you got that backwards, sis. He's not supposed to see me."

"Oh yeah." Talia looked her up and down again with awe. "He's going to die you look so beautiful. Yep, he'll keel right over."

Daisy stepped slowly forward, careful not to walk on her dress. "Thanks for being here. I'm so glad we came back together." Once Daisy had gotten over her concerns with Cannon about being number one, she'd taken a look at her life and realized a lot of the problems between her and Talia were simple jealousy. Daisy had called, apologized, and since then they'd been best friends.

Talia looked like she might cry. "I'm just glad my big sister is a bigger person than me. You've always been such a bright spot to everyone around you. I'm sorry we—"

"No sorrows today," said Daisy. "I love you, sis."

"Love you too," said Talia, hugging her. "Now let's get you down there and get you married before that SEAL of yours decides to come find you on a rescue mission."

Marrying Cannon. Nothing had ever sounded better in the whole world. Not even the Best Editor award that was hanging back on the wall that would soon be *their* wall.

Talia gathered up her train and Daisy started walking. The place had an elevator so she didn't even have to try to negotiate the stairs.

As soon as she stepped out, she could see the gathering outside. No one had noticed her yet.

Pasha was standing by the back door with her father, Rasmus Gold. Who ever thought Daisy Close would have not one, but two billionaires at her wedding? Pasha wore a white tulle dress that matched Daisy's but was more simple. The bodice was layered pleated flowers decorated with lace appliqués and crystals. The gown from there down was tulle and lace. Both dresses had trains, but Daisy's flared wider and was much longer. Her bodice was more form-fitting and off the shoulders.

"Hey, Appassionata," said Daisy.

When the little girl turned, her eyes grew as wide as platters.

"Daisy Mae, you look beautiful!" She ran forward and buried herself in Daisy's gown.

"You do too, little sister. Are you ready?"

"Yes I am. Thank you for inviting me to be your ring bearer."

"I'm so glad you could make it." To Mr. Gold, she said, "Thank you for coming, and thank you again for my beautiful dress." It had been their wedding present, and Daisy couldn't even guess how much it cost.

"It's my pleasure," he said in his unplaceable accent. "Pasha and I wish you and Cannon the very, very best." It was easy to see where his daughter got her manners from.

Daisy and Talia made their way outside, to where their father was waiting behind a wall that obscured him from the rest of the patio. He took a good look at her, and said, "Oh Daisy. I'm so happy for you."

She hugged him, so happy he was here. Things had improved in her relationship with her parents recently as well.

"Go time?" asked Talia.

Daisy nodded, scared to speak.

Talia gave her one more hug and whispered, "Don't forget, I want you to help me find a SEAL as soon as you get back from your honeymoon."

Daisy chuckled as her sister walked over to the DJ, then made her way to the front. Most of Cannon's SEAL buddies were getting snatched up recently. There was something in the water around here. Or maybe after Corbin started it all, they felt like they had to follow suit to feel like part of the team. Either way, Daisy would do what she could to get her sister hooked up.

The day was perfect, low 70s, some cloud cover, a fresh breeze rolling in off the ocean bringing a fresh salty scent. The wedding march started up and Daisy felt a rush of excitement. She wanted to dance up the aisle to her man, but forced herself to walk in a measured pace at her father's side.

Cannon was waiting for her, smiling bigger than she'd ever seen. He was clean shaven and wearing a tuxedo that made him look like an international spy. But it was his eyes that she loved the most. Those emerald green eyes that looked at her with such focus and love. Daisy never had to worry about a single thing with him in her life.

Talia, and the other bridesmaids were lined up on one side: Maia, her college roommate, River's new bride Ally, and Corbin's wife Delaney. On the other side stood all of Cannon's buddies: River, Zane, Blayze, and Corbin. He had refused to pick a best man among them.

Her eyes went back to Cannon, and she wasn't even tempted to make up a fantasy story in her head. Nothing could ever be better than this.

Before she knew it, she was at Cannon's side, and her father handed her off. The men shook hands, and he took a seat in the front row next to Daisy's mom.

Cannon winked at her and Daisy just wanted to run off alone with him, but she forced herself to face Pastor Riley, a man she'd grown to know well through Cannon's involvement as a lay pastor. The ministry plans were going perfectly. It would launch officially in a month.

The wedding was planned to be short, and passed in a blur. All she remembered was cute little Pasha coming up the aisle with the rings on a pillow and one line from Cannon's vows.

"You are the most important thing in my life, and I'll never ring the bell."

Oh, and she would never forget looking into her real fiancé's eyes and saying, "I do."

"... now pronounce you man and wife."

That was it! That's what she'd been waiting for.

Apparently, Cannon had too because even though he'd been staring at her, he snapped to attention, grabbed her and dipped her into a kiss—firm and soft, protective yet demanding. Warrior and lover. The kiss was everything he was and she wanted all of him forever and ever.

When they finally came up for air, they were still staring into each other's eyes. She said, "We should probably go meet our guests, my real husband."

"What guests?" he said with a wink. "The only one I see here is you."

He kissed her again and Daisy kissed him back, so happy for this fantasy her life had become.

THE END

NAVY SEAL ROMANCE SERIES

Read the other Navy SEAL Romance books today!

(Another round of Navy SEAL Romances comes out Fall of 2018!)

~

The Resolved Warrior by Jennifer Youngblood

The Protective Warrior by Cami Checketts

The Peaceful Warrior by Daniel Banner

The Honorable Warrior by Kimberly Krey

The Broken Warrior by Taylor Hart

The Reckless Warrior by Jennifer Youngblood

The Captivating Warrior by Cami Checketts and Daniel Banner

ABOUT THE AUTHOR

Daniel Banner, a 17-year fireman and paramedic, collects experiences by day and makes up stories by nights, and sometimes vice versa. For Daniel, writing is an escape from the traumatic days, and a celebration of the triumphant days.

ALSO BY DANIEL BANNER

Navy SEAL Romance Series
    The Peaceful Warrior
    The Captivating Warrior

Park City Firefighter Romance Series
    Two Hearts Rescue
    A Perfect Rescue
    Rescue and Redemption

Park City Firefighter Romance Series: Station Two
    Sparks Will Fly

Kisses and Commitment Series
    How to Find a Keeper

My Heart Channel Romance Series

9 Reasons to Fall in Love

Made in the USA
Columbia, SC
14 July 2019